Strange Reunion

"So this is how you wrote your messages." Mike laughed, and my breath caught in my throat. He was gorgeous when he laughed. "You beat them with a paper clip. God, I love you, Angel. A paper clip." He laughed again.

I stood still, overwhelmed by a memory. *Mike handing me a small, slim box at Christmastime. Opening it and seeing the necklace glittering within. And crying. Crying, because although the angel was beautiful, it wasn't what I'd wanted for Christmas.*

I'd wanted the words. Even though I'd known how Mike felt about me, I'd wanted the words.

And now my heart shattered over finally hearing him say, "I love you"—

—and not being able to say the words back.

Books by Nicole Luiken

Violet Eyes
Silver Eyes

Available from Pocket Pulse

Published by Pocket Books

SILVER EYES

a novel by

Nicole Luiken

POCKET PULSE
New York London Toronto Sydney Singapore

An *Original* Publication of POCKET BOOKS

POCKET PULSE published by
Pocket Books, a division of Simon & Schuster, Inc.
1230 Avenue of the Americas, New York, NY 10020

ISBN: 0-7434-0078-X

First Pocket Pulse printing December 2001

10 9 8 7 6 5 4 3 2 1

POCKET PULSE and colophon are trademarks of
Simon & Schuster, Inc.

For information regarding special discounts for bulk purchases, please
contact Simon & Schuster Special Sales at 1-800-456-6798 or
business@simonandschuster.com

Front cover illustration and design by Jeanne M. Lee;
photo credit: Tony Stone Images

Printed in the U.S.A.

For my son, Simon, who was born during
the writing of this book

Acknowledgments

I would like to thank the following members of my writers' group for their help and encouragement: Aaron Humphrey, Ann Marston, Karen Glessing, Kevin Lotsberg, Mari Bergen, Marissa Kochanski, Marg De Marco, and Susan McFadzen.

SILVER
EYES

CHAPTER

1

I NOTICED THE FIRST serious gap in my memory eleven days after my training accident.

Before that, the memory lapses had been just small things: forgetting what high school I'd attended, blanking on who gave me my angel pendant. Little things that nagged at me when I tried to sleep at night but that I forgot during the day.

Until I found a secret message wadded up in the toe of my sock.

I almost didn't read it. I was running a little behind schedule for my morning workout, and my instructor hated people to be late. Anaximander would be ten minutes early for his own death. I, however, was of the opinion that if Anaximander wanted me in the gym at 6:20 A.M. he should say, "Angel, be there at 6:20 A.M.," not 6:30 A.M.

Every morning I played a little game with myself, seeing if I could arrive exactly on time, neither early nor late, preventing a lecture from Anaximander while still annoying him.

I was already a couple of minutes late when my big toe encountered something in my sock. Impatiently, I yanked off the sock and pulled out the offending object.

I was about to throw it away when I noticed that it was a piece of paper neatly folded into a square, not a piece of lint as I had assumed. Frowning, I opened it. Pinholes in the paper spelled out three words: "Violet eyes lie."

For half an instant I knew what the words meant—and then the world flipped on me. *Dropping through murky green water like a stone. My hands and legs thrashing and struggling, but not bringing me closer to the surface. Pressure in my lungs, stopped breath; water getting darker and colder as I fall away from the light—*

An eyeblink and I was back in my plain all-white bedroom at SilverDollar.

I hated it when that happened. Really, really hated it.

I took a deep breath, swallowing back the thick nausea that had risen in my throat. I rubbed my hands down my sweatpants. My hands were damp, but my clothes weren't. See? I told myself. You're safe and dry. You're not drowning.

Grimly, I forced myself to look back down at the message—"Violet eyes lie"—but its meaning now frustrated me.

I hurried into the tiny bathroom and washed away the greasy sweat that had sprung up on my skin. I sluiced the meager cup of water dispensed by the conservation sink over my face and stared at my reflection. My eyes were a purple-blue that could be called violet. Was the message calling me a liar? Why? I couldn't remember telling any lies lately—nothing major anyway. Telling Anaximander I'd eaten a bran muffin, when actually I'd eaten a doughnut, didn't count.

I couldn't *remember* lying, but what if I had and just didn't remember? A cold talon of fear scratched down my spine at the possibility.

I reread the message a third time. "Violet eyes lie." The message seemed vaguely hostile to me, a threat.

But if it was a threat sent by some unknown enemy, why hide it in such an inobvious place, where it might never be found? Why not send an anonymous e-mail? Or write it in bloodred lipstick on the mirror if e-mail wasn't dramatic enough?

Secrecy was the only reason I could think of to hide the message. The sender of the message had wanted to be sure that I, and nobody else, found it.

I automatically picked up a Clean-comb and started running it through my short blond hair, trying in vain to think of someone who might have left such a message. I'd been employed by the SilverDollar Mining Company for only two weeks, and, other than Anaximander, I knew only a few other employees casually. People to sit with at lunch or shoot a few hoops with after work. At eighteen I was SilverDollar's youngest employee by a good six years, which kind of inhibited instant friendships.

I tried to picture Anaximander breaking into my room to leave mysterious messages in my sock drawer, but the image wouldn't gel. Anaximander was far too dignified.

I put down the comb, my hair now clean and shiny after having been de-oiled by the Clean-comb, but my expression was unhappy. Reluctantly, I faced the truth. I knew who had sent the message, and it wasn't Anaximander. I had recognized the note's handwriting as soon as I'd seen it.

I had written it.

I tried to convince myself that it was impossible to identify handwriting made up of pinpricks, but I couldn't. The *t* had been crossed at a jaunty angle, and the top of the *s* was smaller than the bottom, both traits of mine. The message had been written by me, Angel Eastland, and not only had I forgotten what it meant, I couldn't remember writing it in the first place.

Not good.

I touched the bandage on my forehead, and the blond girl in the mirror did the same. I had no memory of the training accident in which I'd hurt myself, but the doctor had told me that spot amnesia wasn't unusual with head injuries so I hadn't been concerned. But this was more than spot amnesia. Chilled, I wondered what else I had forgotten. Something important?

Something dangerous?

A sick feeling rode low in my stomach. Something was very wrong inside my own head.

The correct thing to do at that point would have been to go to the infirmary to tell Dr. Clark about not remembering the message, but something inside me balked. My breath came quicker as if I was afraid. Why didn't I want to go to the doctor?

Five seconds later a soothing, plausible reason

occurred to me. I couldn't go to the doctor even if I wanted to; it was too early in the morning. My pulse eased up.

I looked at my watch, saw that I was late for my workout with Anaximander, and slammed out the door.

Four steps down the hall, I stopped, compelled to go back for the note. The door to my quarters had a cardlock, and the only thing likely to enter my room while I was gone was the housecleaning robot that came through the vents under my bed, but I felt better with the message in my pocket.

I sprinted down the red- and white-tiled halls, going from the Blue Section, where staff quarters were, past Gray (Work), and into Yellow Section (Exercise and Recreation). I stopped running once I turned down the last hallway so my breathing was under control when I arrived.

Anaximander frowned at me. "Angel, you're late. On the job, timing is everything." He saw nothing ironic about wasting the next ten minutes lecturing me for being six minutes late.

Although it was notoriously hard to read Augmented people, Anaximander didn't seem to possess a sense of humor or much in the way of emotions at all. A tall black man with a shaved head, he rarely smiled, and his silver eyes, with their Augmented vision, gave nothing away.

I briefly considered confiding in him but decided against it. Anaximander spent a couple of hours a day training me to be a security investigator as he was, and did a diligent job, but I was always aware that he was also testing me to see if I was worth SilverDollar's money.

There was no one at SilverDollar I could confide in.

I fought against the current of homesickness that threatened to sweep me away. I focused on Anaximander; he had information I needed. "How did I hurt my head?" I asked.

Anaximander stopped, thrown off balance by the abrupt change of subject. "You fell."

Had I imagined a slight pause before he spoke? "Fell from where? Were you with me?"

"A rope. We were rope climbing."

I accepted that in silence, but the answer felt unsatisfying, sparking no memories.

"Being late is also unprofessional." Anaximander picked up his lecture where he'd left off.

My mind wandered. Why had the message been written in pinpricks? Hadn't I had access to a pen?

"Okay, let's get started," Anaximander said long minutes later.

We did stretches and warm-up exercises for ten minutes. Anaximander had Augments in his legs, which meant that he could run me and any other un-Augmented person into the ground, but I was a lot more flexible than he was. I usually took pleasure in proving it, sitting and bending forward until my head touched the floor, but today the rote exercises irritated me. I was dying to get back to my room to examine the message again, maybe do a computer search on "Violet eyes lie."

"Enough warm-up," Anaximander said. "Let's go outside and do a five-mile run."

The restless thing inside me sat up and howled at the thought of yet another run. Boring, boring, boring. "Why?"

Anaximander turned his silver-eyed stare on me like a weapon. "Running is an excellent cardiovascular exercise."

I cut him off. "No. I mean, why do I have to be in such great shape? What does it have to do with my job?" From what I'd been told, a security investigator acted like a troubleshooter, an outsider sent in to figure out what was causing the problem with a mining operation.

For a moment I thought I'd stumped Anaximander, but then he said smoothly, "Your fitness training is in case something goes wrong on the job. If you uncover some saboteurs, your life may depend on being able to run five miles faster than they can."

I didn't buy it. Did neither I, nor the hypothetical saboteurs, have an aircar? But I didn't argue the point because it gave me an opportunity to twist things to my advantage. "Running while being chased is different from just running. Let's practice chasing!" I threw excitement into my voice.

Anaximander was unmoved. He crossed his arms. "What do you have in mind?"

I noticed that the other employees using the gym were looking our way, curious. I pitched my idea to them. "The maze. One of us chases the other into the maze. We each carry a volleyball. The first to either nail the opponent or reach the exit wins."

Grins and encouraging comments broke out.

"Sounds like fun."

"You show her, Anaximander!"

"I'll race you if he won't."

I raised a challenging eyebrow at Anaximander. "Well?"

"Throwing a volleyball isn't very similar to taking down an opponent," he observed.

I shrugged. "Okay. No volleyballs. We pretend that we have Knockout patches, and we try to tag each other. Are we on?"

A cool nod. "Yes. Who goes first? The person being chased has the advantage."

I was feeling generous. "I'll chase you. You can have a ten-second head start."

The maze was in one of the gardens surrounding SilverDollar's facility. I'd jogged past it with Anaximander but never gone inside. The walls were concrete, eight feet high, and covered with murals of mining scenes. Very tacky.

Most of our audience followed us outside, tracking through the dewy grass, and I chose Ben, a thin, dark-bearded techie whom I'd played basketball with, to stand as timekeeper.

"Wait," I said, just as Anaximander was about to enter. I smiled at him. "Care to make a bet on the outcome?"

He shook his head. "I don't bet."

"Anyone else?" I looked hopefully at Ben.

"You're hell on wheels on the basketball court," Ben said. "I'd bet on you if you were going first, but no way can you win going second. I've seen you two run together." Ben politely didn't mention Anaximander's many Augments, which would help him.

"It's a bet then," I said, swinging my arms to keep the muscles loose in the April morning chill.

"Winner gets to use the loser's employee debit card for one day."

The others whistled appreciatively.

Ben insisted on a maximum spending allowance but accepted the bet. I tried not to show my relief. The bet was the best way that I'd thought of to get my hands on someone else's debit card.

Anaximander looked impatient. "Can we start now?"

Ben clicked his stopwatch. "Go!"

Anaximander vanished into the maze. I listened for his footsteps but heard only a faint patter. I couldn't tell which way he'd gone.

Ten seconds ticked by. "Go!" Ben shouted.

I entered the maze at a crouched run. The entrance bottleneck was the most obvious place for an ambush, and when I saw movement ahead of me I threw myself into a dive.

On the floor, I saw that it wasn't Anaximander's tall black form up ahead, but my own reflection in a mirror. Only the outside of the maze was painted; inside, all the walls were mirrored, throwing off infinities of possible turns. It took my eyes a moment to sort out the two true choices available to me: left, then straight ahead or right, then straight ahead.

Anaximander could follow two possible strategies: running flat out for the exit or lying in ambush. It all depended on whether or not he knew the maze. I didn't see Anaximander as the type to be intrigued by a maze, but if he had walked through it even once he would be able to call up the layout from his Memory Recorder Augment and navigate it perfectly. If he didn't know the maze, he risked losing time in a cul-de-sac and being tagged by me when he reversed, so ambush was the better option.

If so, he was sure to be waiting just beyond one of the passages. If I chose wrongly, he'd tag me as soon as I poked my head around the corner. If I chose correctly the game would become more complicated with the two of us hunting each other.

My odds of winning were less than fifty percent. I've always hated losing. So I changed the rules.

CHAPTER

2

I FACED THE INNER WALL of the maze and jumped up. My hands caught the top edge of the mirrored wall, and I exhaled softly, trying not to grunt as I pulled myself up out of the maze.

The walls were six inches wide; no sweat for someone who'd had her own balance beam as a kid. From above I scoped out the layout of the maze: the right-hand path led to a dead end, while the left-hand one eventually wound around to the exit.

I spotted Anaximander running down the correct path, halfway through the maze.

"Hey!" One of the crowd at the exit saw me and pointed. After a jaunty wave, I ignored them, intent on the maze.

I started to run along the top of the wall but quickly realized I couldn't catch up to Anaximander without going too fast and risking a bad fall. And losing.

I narrowed my eyes and took a closer look at

the maze, memorizing the hairpin turns and forks that led to the exit. Swiftly, I lowered myself back down to the ground. I took off at a run, taking the next three turns flat out. Left, right, right again.

The correct path went left next, but I kept running straight forward into a dead end. I charged my own reflection, leaping at the wall. I scrambled over it into the passageway beyond, saving myself a lengthy detour. Unfortunately, I was still behind Anaximander.

A second scramble over another wall did the trick. I was home free, within sight of the exit, when a sudden impulse of mischief seized me. Anaximander would be confident of victory, certain that even if I could catch him, I would come up from behind. Never in a million years would he expect me to have gotten ahead of him.

Ben poked his head into the maze, impatient to see who the winner would be, and I held a finger to my lips for silence. I flattened myself against the last corner.

I almost forgot about my reflection, but a movement from Ben in one of the mirrors reminded me. I retreated two steps, pulling my mirror image with me, just as Anaximander's footsteps pounded up.

The second his reflection entered the mirror facing me, I launched myself forward. I slapped his arm.

"Tag! You're It," I started to say, but Anaximander cut the words off in my throat, grabbing my arm and twisting it behind my back. His arm hooked around my neck—and then loosened as he remembered that this was a friendly contest, not a true pursuit. He released me, and for a moment I saw astonishment on his face. "How did you get ahead of me?"

Ben answered. "She climbed over a couple of walls. She beat you to the exit, too, but went back for the double win." He shook his head in disbelief. "I bet on the wrong person."

I grinned.

Anaximander wasn't impressed. As we exited the maze, he said coldly, "You cheated. The purpose of the chase was to test your fitness. You circumvented this."

His words stole all the pleasure from my victory. I shrugged, trying to hide my hurt. "I thought the purpose of the exercise was to win." Which I had.

He paused, then softened his stance. "You demonstrated great ingenuity. Nevertheless, I wished to test your abilities. We will repeat the exercise—"

"Oh, surely there's no need for that," a new voice said.

I turned and saw a short, little man with black hair and sideburns walking toward us. He wore a skintight gray suit with a purple iridescent sheen, the kind of outfit only the vain and rich wore and only the young and beautiful *should* wear. It threatened to burst at the seams when he flexed his biceps.

Ben and the other watchers scattered as he neared us, as if suddenly remembering other places they had to be.

"I was watching the contest from the second floor; Angel here seems very competent to me." He showed off his dental work with a smile, but the warmth didn't reach his close-set brown eyes. "I'm Edward Castellan, but please call me Eddy."

I blinked once, then shook his manicured hand. His heavy gold ring pressed into my palm. I recognized the name of SilverDollar's Head of Operations. Eddy? I was supposed to call him Eddy? "Nice to meet you," I said politely.

"That was very impressive, Angel. We're glad to have you on our team." Up close, the tightness of his skin made me suspect that his muscles were from body-sculpting surgery, not anything as sweaty as exercise. "I think she's ready to go on a real job, don't you, Anaximander?"

When your boss suggests something you agree. "Very soon," Anaximander stalled.

"Why wait?" Eddy said, still smiling, but with a hard edge to his voice. "Why don't you take her along on the case you're working on?"

I pricked up my ears, interested in spite of the bad vibes the two of them were giving off. I hadn't realized Anaximander was working on an investigation during the hours I spent doing lessons.

"I don't think this is the right case for Angel to start with," Anaximander said.

"I insist. After all, you could use the help!" Eddy smiled as if making a joke, but I got an uneasy feeling that it wasn't funny. "How long has the fugitive been eluding you now?"

"Five months, sir." Anaximander's voice was toneless, but something in his body language raised the hair on the back of my neck. He staggered slightly as if standing on the deck of a ship in stormy seas. He blinked—a purely habitual function as his silver eyes had no need of lubrication. He watched Eddy as a hypnotized bird might watch a snake.

Seriously creeped out, I followed his gaze to where Eddy was fiddling with a bizarre necklace he wore instead of a tie. A black, butterfly-shaped piece of plastic, three inches tall, that dangled from a black cord. The plastic had something engraved on it, but Eddy's fingers hid all but the first two letters, *A L.*

"Well, I'm sure you'll catch him soon," Eddy said, a definite implied threat in his tone. *Catch him soon, or else.* "I have confidence in you, Anaximander. You're our best investigator. At least until Angel here starts!" He clapped me on the shoulder, laughing heartily.

What a loser.

"So how are you doing, Angel?" Eddy asked. "Are you settling in here at SilverDollar?"

There's something wrong with my memory, I thought but didn't say. "Everything's great. I'm enjoying working here."

"Let me know if there's anything I can do to help. Anything, anytime, okay?" He winked.

"I will," I lied.

After another minute of uncomfortable small talk, Eddy turned back to Anaximander. "I'm sure I'll hear from you soon. When you catch the fugitive."

A small bead of sweat had formed on Anaximander's forehead. Amazing. I would have sworn he was too Augmented to still have sweat glands.

"Yes, sir." Anaximander's gaze remained locked on the token around Eddy's neck.

What could it be? A good luck charm? It was rather large and clunky. It didn't go with the corporate image.

Eddy nodded to us both and left. We stared after him for several moments in silence. I noticed that he had tiny feet.

Eddy. I couldn't get over the little-boy nickname. Had he been trying to be buddies? Puhleeze.

I gave in to my curiosity. "What was he wearing around his neck?"

Anaximander shuddered as if coming out of a trance. "What?"

"The thing around his neck. What was it?"

"I don't know. I didn't notice it." Anaximander began to walk back to the gym.

I stared after him, unable to tell from his enigmatic expression whether or not he was lying. I caught up with him at the door, before he could vanish for the day. "Tell me about this fugitive we're after." I didn't like the way Eddy had forced my help on Anaximander, implying that he was incompetent, but I couldn't help feeling a rush of anticipation. I was dying to get out of the classroom and do something. "Is it a saboteur?"

"No, a thief. He has something that belongs to SilverDollar that's worth millions."

"Do you know where he is?" I trotted at Anaximander's side down the hallway.

"I've narrowed down the area," Anaximander said precisely.

I raised an eyebrow, waiting.

"He was last seen in Taber two days ago."

"So close?" I asked, astonished. Taber was only

twenty kilometers away. I would have expected the thief to leave the province of Alberta, if not the entire continent-country of NorAm. Staying so close to SilverDollar's Operations facility was either an act of idiocy or great daring, hiding in plain sight.

Anaximander nodded tersely. "He wants something we have. Until he gets it, he's not going anywhere. I have a dozen men conducting a door-to-door search. He'll be found soon."

If he had eluded Anaximander, the most tenacious person I knew, for months, I didn't think we could count on him turning up on a door-to-door search.

Taber. I cast my mind back to a map of the area I'd seen.

"You know," I said, "if it were me, the Wasteland is where I'd go." The stretch of barren land—once prosperous corn farmland—had been devastated by a man-made blight during the World Environmental Crisis. In the years since the crisis, eighty percent of arable land had been successfully reclaimed, but Taber's soil was one of the unlucky varieties that the process didn't work on. Now it was good only for collecting solar energy.

"Impossible," Anaximander said flatly. "On sunny days the solar collectors are too hot. It would be like hiding in a frying pan. He would go blind from the mirror glare."

A dart of annoyance pierced me. "The fact that it's impossible just makes it safe. I'll bet I could do it, and if I could, so could he."

"No."

"If I'm right, one of the solar collectors will be

registering slightly less energy than the rest of them," I said.

Wordlessly, Anaximander moved to one of the numerous computer access points that dotted the complex. I watched over his shoulder as a hologram of blue hexes appeared. "There." I pointed at a border hexagon that was shaded more green than blue. "That hex. Off by one and a half percent."

"It could be anything," Anaximander said. "A dead bird. A spot of rust."

"It's him. I know it."

"So confident." Anaximander stared at me for a moment. "All right. This afternoon we'll search the solar collectors. Do your morning lessons, and then meet me at the aircar bay at one o'clock."

I grinned at Anaximander's departing back. Yes! My first assignment!

Back in my room, I changed clothes. Before dropping the exercise sweats on the floor for the housecleaning robots to launder, I carefully transferred the note to my white pants.

"Violet eyes lie." I had written those words. What did they mean?

Lie to whom? About what?

I was starving, but that wasn't why I hotfooted it over to the cafeteria. Ben was just finishing his breakfast when I arrived. He groaned when he saw me but paid for my stack of pancakes.

I snatched the debit card out of his hand when he would have pocketed it again. "That's mine, I believe. Now what was that spending limit again?" I teased. "A hundred and fifty dollars? Two hundred?"

"Fifty!" Ben was on his feet, reaching for the card.

I laughed and eluded his grasp. "Okay, fifty it is. See you at lunch." I waved him off.

After wolfing down my breakfast, I put in an hour doing lessons. Learning by computer was faster than classroom learning, but one hundred times duller. No other students to joke around with, no teacher to lure off topic . . . no one to tattle when I skipped out. I usually whipped through four modules a day in an effort to impress Anaximander, but since he had failed so far to notice my diligence I figured he wouldn't notice today's absence either.

I made it safely back to my quarters without encountering anyone and lost no time doing a computer database search on "Violet eyes lie."

If the message I had received was secret or dangerous in some way, using Ben's employee card instead of my own would prevent the search from showing up as a debit on my payroll statement. The precaution was probably unnecessary, but it made me feel better.

One hundred thirteen sites.

I screened through the first twenty article summaries, but none of them contained all three of my search terms so I paid for a full-text download. It brought me within sixteen dollars of the limit Ben had insisted on, but I had to know.

While the computer completed the download, I paced the room. My white bedroom and tiny bathroom looked plain and bare, incapable of concealing anything. Compelled, I searched my sock drawer for more secret messages. I felt slightly silly when my labors produced only a handful of lint, but not silly enough to stop myself from searching the rest of my clothes.

I had almost given up when I found another scrap of paper deep in a decorative pocket of my blue jeans. Before I read the pinprick message, I examined the paper it was written on. One edge was torn, and when I took out the "Violet eyes lie" message, the two pieces of paper matched up. It was a receipt for potatoes, not exactly helpful. A third of it was still missing; there must be at least one more message.

The message on the other side spelled "Renaissance."

Renaissance referred to a time in European history when there was a great flourishing of the arts and sciences, but the image that popped into my mind when I read it was of a hairy Neanderthal man.

And then I was drowning again for the second time that day. *Cold water closing over my head; my boots dragging me down into the dark green depths.*

When I surfaced again, I put my hand on the wall to steady myself. My pulse thundered in my neck. By the time I stopped being scared, I was angry. Why the hell did that keep happening?

In my mind, I went back over the times the drowning memory had overtaken me—eight times in all. I came to the disquieting realization that the episodes hadn't started until after my training accident. Worse, they usually happened when I was trying to remember something and failing. The puzzle was that I couldn't remember ever drowning either. In fact, I was positive I could swim.

The computer flashed blue, signaling that the download was complete.

I skimmed through the first one hundred articles the computer had pulled up but failed to find anything significant. Usually the words *violet, eyes,* and *lie* were separated by a lot of text and were totally unrelated.

I was about to skip over an article titled "Movie Sets the Fashion: Violet Eyes In," when a word farther down caught my eye. "Renaissance." The second secret message I'd found. "The movie *Escape from History* is based on the true-life story of Project Renaissance." Frustratingly, after that the article went back to talking about fashion. The last twelve articles were duds.

I took the results of my first search and added in the term *Renaissance*. One site only, the article I'd already read. Then I tried searching for *Project Renaissance* and hit the jackpot: 20,529 hits. Too many to look through.

With only eleven dollars left on Ben's debit card, I was faced with the choice of downloading a random sample of Project Renaissance articles, which might or might not be relevant, or downloading *Escape from History*. I picked the movie.

Mistake. *Escape from History* had a rating of one and a half stars out of five. In my opinion, they'd given it one star too many. It sucked.

Pallid blonde, who looks too old to still be in high school, is supersmart and is picked on by her 1950s-era classmates. Hunky guy moves to town and romances her, then vanishes. Everybody in town pretends they never met him. Blond girl discovers that the reason she's supersmart is that she's the result of an illegal genetic experiment called Project Renaissance. Scientists have been watching her from hidden cameras her whole life, the 1950s town where she lives is fake, and the year is actually 2098. She escapes and tracks down her boyfriend only to find out that he was part of the setup. He never loved her; the evil scientists hired him to get her pregnant. The movie ends with her supersmart baby being taken away from her to be raised in the fake 1950s town where she'd started out.

By the end of the movie, I wanted to slap the main character. She'd spent half the movie either in tears or screaming hysterically. If she was so supersmart, why had it taken her so long to figure out that her boyfriend was a scuzzball? His name, Judas, ought to have been a clue.

It was a stupid movie, but it scared the hell out of me. Because the blond girl's name was Angel, and she had violet eyes. And the cardboard 1950s town and hidden cameras had struck a chord.

I had a terrible feeling that the Angel in the movie was supposed to be me.

Which was ridiculous. I did well at school— okay, very well—but I wasn't genetically engineered to be supersmart like the blonde in the movie. Or at least I didn't think so. The truth was, without classmates to compare myself to, I couldn't judge how intelligent I was. I tried not to think about how easily I'd outwitted Anaximander in the maze.

The whole movie was so hokey I couldn't tell what was based on truth and what was pure Hollywood. I was willing to believe that Project Renaissance had been a real genetic experiment aimed at creating supersmart people, but I still didn't know what "Violet eyes lie" meant. The blonde had been lied to, but had told no lies herself.

I gave Ben back his debit card at lunch and paid for my own sandwich. I sat by myself and didn't attempt any conversation. Even after lunch, I was still so rattled I forgot to play my little head game and actually arrived at the aircar hangar at 12:50 P.M., the same time that Anaximander did.

"Ready to go, I see," Anaximander said. If he was pleased, I couldn't tell.

"Ready to catch the bad guy." A sudden thought occurred to me. "What's the fugitive's name, anyhow?"

"Michael Vallant."

In my mind I saw the face of a good-looking, dark-haired boy.

And then the image pitched me back into the drowning memory: *falling through green water, arms flailing helplessly, sinking—*

CHAPTER

3

I WAS GASPING FOR BREATH when I tore free of the memory, as if I really had been drowning. I wouldn't have been surprised to find my clothes soaking wet, the sensation had been so real.

"Angel?" Anaximander was looking at me funny.

I faked up a smile. "It's nothing."

"Then let's go."

My smile slid off my face as soon as his back was turned. I shuddered. The drowning memory always made me feel horribly vulnerable.

"We're taking the Black Panther," Anaximander said a moment later.

Exhilaration blew away the lingering cobwebs of fear. "SilverDollar has a Black Panther?" Black Panthers were state-of-the-art aircars.

"Yes," Anaximander said. "Mr. Castellan likes to have all the newest toys."

The sleek, bullet-nosed craft was capable of speeds that scared any thinking person; as soon as I saw it my hands itched to take the controls.

To my surprise, Anaximander let me sit in the pilot's seat. "Go ahead," he said expressionlessly. "Take her up."

It was another test. I had been studying for my pilot's license, had spent hours flying—in virtual reality simulations. The Black Panther had a few extra controls. Fortunately, I had been watching the other times Anaximander had flown us so I knew how to start the engine. It purred smoothly under my hands.

I glanced at Anaximander, but he said nothing, waiting.

There was no way I was going to ask what to do next. He would tell me quick enough if I did anything wrong.

Fortunately, aircars were as close to idiot-proof as could be made. The computer called out the preflight checks, and I verified that all the gauges were lit and reading correctly.

"Please set course," the computer said in my ear. I was wearing a headset, but Anaximander had an Earradio Augment and didn't need one.

"The Wasteland." I named the specific solar hex that was our destination.

A minute passed while the Panther's computer consulted Alberta Air Traffic Control to lay in a course and altitude that would not cross anybody else's flight path.

"Flight path laid in," the computer said.

I switched on the AutoTakeoff, and the Black Panther rose straight up in the air. The aircar's vertical takeoff never failed to put a grin on my face.

I hung onto the control yoke out of habit, but the computer did the flying.

The Black Panther accelerated smoothly instead of blasting forward the way I would have preferred, but the Wasteland was so close we'd barely started when we arrived.

Destination reached, the AutoPilot beeped, and the Panther went into a circling pattern at 914 meters. The computer polarized the cockpit windows against the blinding mirror glare from below.

"Shall I land?" I asked Anaximander. My fingers hovered over the AutoLanding switch.

"Yes, but do it manually. We don't want the engine noise to alert the fugitive." Anaximander reached over and turned off the ignition.

The four powerful engines faltered and then died.

The aircar bucked and bobbed, starting to fall and hitting air turbulence on the way down.

My heart stuttered and fell along with it. I pulled up hard on the control yoke, but without the engine power behind the aircar, we still fell. Glide landings had been covered in my VR simulations, but I'd spent most of my time practicing loops and barrel rolls and other fancy tricks. I hadn't spent much time on the basics.

In VR, glide landings had seemed boring. Real life was a bit different. *We were falling.* My mouth dried.

Anaximander crossed his arms and watched me, seemingly unconcerned at our plummeting.

Pride rescued me from panic. Anaximander was in the copilot's seat. If I screwed up, he could take over in a blink.

Besides, we were 914 meters above the ground.

I glanced at the gauge. Make that 823 meters and gaining speed.

The aircar had only short stubby wings, but it had several flaps and extensions that I could deploy to increase my wingspan. After a frantic twenty-second hunt while we kept dropping like a stone, I found the correct buttons. The extensions, made of ultralight ultrastrong materials, snapped out, jolting the aircar, and this time when I pulled up on the control yoke our descent slowed.

I drew in a shaky breath. So far so good.

I turned the control yoke to the left, sending us into a lazy spiral, then, once the direction had been established, returned the control yoke to the neutral position.

More turbulence shook the Black Panther, but I managed to keep the nose fairly steady.

Okay, I'd slowed our descent. Now I needed a place to land. According to its specs, the Black Panther needed only 250 meters of runway to do a glide landing. Since the solar panel hexagons were half a kilometer in diameter I ought to be able to land the Panther with a whole 250 meters to spare.

It sounded easy. If I'd practiced on the simulations more it might even have *been* easy. Unfortunately, this was the part that I'd crashed my aircar on four times in VR. I'd landed correctly twice in a row, then blithely decided to go on to more interesting stuff.

Oops.

"I'm going to land in the hex to the northeast of the fugitive's hideout," I told Anaximander. "Starting on my approach."

The wind was blowing from north, northeast at twenty-five kilometers per hour. In order to land with the nose into the wind, I would have to angle across one side of the hexagon, reducing my runway by about a hundred feet.

Anaximander didn't tell me to try again, or reach for the controls, so I gritted my teeth and landed the aircar.

The wheels touched down, then bounced. I tried again. Another jarring bounce. My 150 meters of insurance was shrinking, the walls of solar panels rushing ever closer.

I wasn't going to be able to stop in time.

"I'm taking over!" Anaximander flipped the switch, giving him control of the aircar as we started to touch down again.

"No!" I yelled. There wasn't enough room to land. I hit Anaximander in the face and flipped the controls back over to me. Then I deliberately bounced the aircar back into the air so that we neatly hopped the wall of solar panels and bumped down on the other side in another hex.

Anaximander was silent as we rolled to a stop.

We were alive, and the Black Panther was still in one piece. Light-headed with relief, I smiled.

My smile set Anaximander off. "You should not have hit me. You could have killed us." No anger showed on his face, but the edge to his voice was the equivalent of a shout from anyone else.

My own temper flared. "We'd have crashed if I hadn't taken back over. There wasn't enough room to land."

"I was going to switch the Vertical Takeoff and Landing back on. And the reason there wasn't room to do a glide landing was because you bounced twice!"

What he said was perfectly true. I should have handed the controls over to Anaximander as soon as I realized how close we were going to cut it. I knew that, but I was irrationally angry with him. "At least I got us down. You're the one who decided to turn my first flight into a damn test!"

Anaximander stared at me for such a long time that I began to feel uncomfortable, as if his silver eyes had lasers that could peel me to the bone. Finally, he said, "What do you mean, your first flight? I know you've been studying for your pilot's license. Every schoolchild takes three years of Pilot Education. It's a required course."

If I'd taken such a course, I couldn't remember it. I didn't say so aloud, though, frightened of betraying the gaps in my memory.

"Have you flown off AutoPilot before?" Anaximander asked.

"I've never flown before, period," I said flatly. "Only VR simulations."

"And it didn't occur to you to tell me this?" Anaximander asked incredulously.

Abruptly, I felt like an idiot. My face burned. "I assumed you knew."

Another long pause and stare. "Next time tell me."

I nodded shortly.

"I'll see that you get more air time," Anaximander said. As we prepared to disembark, he looked at me and shook his head. "First time piloting. Girl, you are terrifying."

He didn't exactly mean it as a compliment, but I

took it that way anyhow. "Thanks." I grinned. I wondered what he would have said if he had known that I had been up in an aircar only five times before in my life, three of them with him. The other two times . . . The gap in my memory widened into an abyss. I couldn't remember them.

A trickle of unease ran down the nape of my neck as I taxied over to the solar wall bordering the hex that was our destination. Black Panthers were rare, but aircars were the major nonurban form of transportation. I was eighteen years old. How could I have ridden in an aircar only twice before coming to work for SilverDollar?

I must not be remembering correctly. And yet part of me was stubbornly sure I was. Five times.

Think about it later, I told myself, and unstrapped my seat belt.

At ground level, the solar panels towered over me, two-story glass-topped boxes set at a sixty-degree slant and arranged in hexagons. Underneath the glass, I could see a corrugated surface designed to keep sunlight from reflecting away. Mirrors lined the base of the hexagons to reflect in more sunlight.

It was impossible to look at the mirrors without raising tears in my eyes and risking blindness. I hastily put on the wraparound sunglasses Anaximander handed me, but even with the lenses polarized as far as they would go, the light was still too bright. I climbed down from the aircar with my eyes closed.

Anaximander's Augmented eyes were impervious to brightness. It would have made more sense to send him in while I watched, but according to Anaximander, the fugitive had no Augments, and I wanted to prove my boastful words that someone could survive in the Wastelands.

There was also the matter of heat. Neither Anaximander nor I was immune to heatstroke, and the temperature was scorching.

Anaximander and I quickly headed for a small break between solar panels, just large enough for a person to squeeze through. We halted in its shade, and I peered forward through slitted eyes.

It was one in the afternoon, and the sun was almost directly overhead. If the fugitive was hiding here, he would be in the thin shade on the opposite side of the hex.

"Still think Michael Vallant is here?" Anaximander asked.

I was beginning to doubt that, but I didn't want to admit it. "Yes."

"I disagree. But just in case you do find him . . . here." He held out an innocuous-looking white square with a loop of thread in one corner. This time he didn't assume. "Have you ever used Knockout medi-patches?"

I shook my head. I'd only seen them in movies. I touched the two-inch square gingerly with one fingernail. "How does it work?"

Anaximander looped a finger through the thread and turned the white square so that the side facing out from his palm had a faint red-stripe pattern on it. "You peel off the protective film"—he demonstrated—"then hit your opponent with it. It doesn't matter where, as long as the patch touches skin. The sedative is absorbed into the bloodstream upon contact. Within ten seconds your opponent will be unconscious." Without warning, he stepped in close and tried to slap the medi-patch on my arm.

"Hey!" I nimbly skipped back out of range.

"As you can see, the weapon has its limitations," Anaximander said, expressionless, as if he had never doubted my ability to pass his test. "It's a weapon of surprise only, a last resort if you get into trouble. If you do find the thief, call me on the headset, and I'll cross over and take him out."

For the first time I felt nervous.

It must have showed on my face. "Are you sure you want to do this?" Anaximander asked after I'd taken the patches.

He expected me to back down. My spine stiff-ened. "Yes. I'm just waiting for that." I pointed at a swiftly moving wisp of cloud overhead. The hex was half a kilometer across. If I were going to cross it without killing myself I would need shade. I had chosen to land on the northeast side of the hex because of the direction of the wind.

Anaximander grunted, silently skeptical.

I charted the shadow cast by the small cloud, and when it drifted overhead, I was ready. I closed my eyes again, took a deep breath, and stepped out into the smothering heat.

I was dressed all in white to help prevent heat-stroke, but it was hard to imagine how black could have been worse. And I was in the shade!

I walked carefully in the direction the cloud had been moving, trying to match its speed and stay under its protective umbrella. I counted steps, rea-soning that about a thousand steps should take me to the other side.

Halfway across, I lost the cloud's shadow.

My eyes snapped open—and were dazzled by the mirror glare. I shut them again, and spots danced on my eyelids.

Blind, I zagged left trying to find the cloud's protection again and failing. I took three more steps forward, caught the leading edge of shadow like a physical touch, and then lost it again. No amount of zigging and zagging after that helped.

A thin wedge of panic drove itself into my brain. Without the shade, it was blazing hot in the center of the mirror. I imagined that the clothes on my body were catching fire in the intense heat, burning up.

I would have to turn around and go back, but which way was back? In my frantic zigzagging I'd lost track.

"There's another cloud coming up. Take five steps to the left." Anaximander's calm voice came over my headset. No lectures this time.

I obeyed gratefully, following his instructions in a strange dance across the mirror. Run forward four steps, zag left one, walk forward, left two, run forward.

"You're at the other side," Anaximander said.

I opened my eyes but left my sunglasses polarized. The west solar wall loomed over me.

The shadow cast by the wall was narrow, almost falling within the sixty-degree slant of the wall itself. At noon the five feet of shade I was standing in might vanish altogether. A person would have to be desperate to hide here.

Nevertheless, my guess had been right. A black tent stood to my right, previously invisible in the mirror's harsh glare.

I looped a Knockout medi-patch over my palm and cat-footed closer. I wanted to be sure that the thief was actually in residence before I radioed Anaximander. I listened outside a moment but could detect no sound from within. It occurred to me that the thief would probably sleep during the intense heat of the day and wake at night.

I decided to peek in.

I depolarized my sunglasses and removed the film from my Knockout patch, then lifted a tiny corner of the tent flap.

A quick glance took in the battery-operated fan, large cooler, and bags of half-melted ice that made the tent bearable. Then I focused on the teenage boy lying on a blanket.

Grinning, I stepped inside, hand held out—and he sat up.

He saw me.

He looked too young to be a million-dollar thief, was my first confused thought, no more than nineteen. In the heat he had removed his shirt and wore only denim cutoffs. His legs were tanned, and his body was lean and athletic. His hair was raven dark, his face strong and handsome—*and his eyes were violet like mine*.

Violet eyes lie.

I recognized him—and then my brain short-circuited, throwing me into the drowning memory, my worst flashback yet.

Plunging down through cold water, murky green at first, but getting darker and colder with every second, every breath not taken—

The drowning memory held me blind and vulnerable. Instinct made me lift the Knockout medi-patch I knew was in my hand though all I could feel was cold water.

My eyes saw only the lightless depths of a watery grave as I slapped out wildly, trying to ward off the thief.

My hand hit flesh, but I wasn't attacked in return.

"Angel!" he exclaimed. "What the hell took you so long? I've been waiting weeks—"

He gave a strangled gasp as the Knockout sedative entered his bloodstream, and when the drowning memory cleared from my vision, he was lying unconscious at my feet.

CHAPTER

4

"HE KNEW MY NAME," I said to Anaximander when he flew over to join me ten minutes later. I felt as pale and shaken as if I truly had drowned. "How did he know my name?"

"He was trying to throw you off," Anaximander said after a pause. "He must have hacked into SilverDollar's personnel files and matched your picture to your face."

I nodded, even though the small tent had no palmtop computer. I said nothing of my own flash of recognition before the drowning memory washed it away. I wanted Anaximander to think I was competent, not crazed.

"So is it here?" I asked. "What does it look like?"

"What does what look like?"

"The thing Michael Vallant stole."

"It's not here." Anaximander sounded certain although he'd barely glanced around the tent. "He'll have hidden it somewhere. Help me carry him to the aircar."

I picked up Michael Vallant's feet, and we carried him to the Panther. All the while, my mind kept churning, trying to figure things out.

"Angel! What the hell took you so long? I've been waiting weeks—"

If he had been waiting for me, it implied that we were partners, that I was also a thief. The thought of stealing from SilverDollar filled me with nausea. It couldn't be true. It must have been a ruse, as Anaximander said.

But what if it was true and I just didn't remember?

After wrestling with the hideous thought during the flight back to SilverDollar's facility, I decided that it didn't matter what I had done before my memory loss. That Angel was a different person.

I prayed that Michael Vallant didn't give me away. Before becoming SilverDollar's employee, I had taken a Loyalty oath that had very strict penalties for deception.

A cordon of guards met us at the aircar hangar when we set down. They took charge of Michael Vallant's limp body.

Anaximander went with them. When I started to follow, he stopped me. "There's no need for you to attend the interrogation. You don't know the particulars of his case so his testimony won't mean anything to you."

I was reluctant to let Michael Vallant out of my sight. "I've never attended a truth-drug interrogation," I said. "I should learn the procedure in case I ever need to use it on the job."

Anaximander frowned. "Another time. You have

a doctor's appointment this afternoon to have your head wound checked."

I opened my mouth to argue some more, but Anaximander cut me off. "Don't worry, I'll give you full credit for the apprehension when I report to Mr. Castellan."

"Eddy," I corrected.

Anaximander gave me a very even look, and I backed down. I didn't want him to think I was trying to impress the boss at his expense. "All right. I'll go see Dr. Clark."

The appointment took a total of fifteen minutes—five of them spent in the waiting room. After a quick look under my bandage, Dr. Clark asked me a few questions. Had I had any headaches? Any dizziness? Truthfully I answered no and avoided mentioning my memory problems.

Outside the infirmary, I looked at my watch and frowned. I could have easily attended the interrogation; obviously Anaximander had simply wished to exclude me.

Why? Did he want to do the interrogation alone to make himself look better when he reported to Eddy? Or did he suspect that Michael Vallant knew me?

Deciding that I was making too much out of the words of a thief, I reluctantly began my next history lesson on the World Environmental Crisis. As usual, I decided to take the test first to see if I needed to bother with the lesson itself.

Question One: In what year did the World Environmental Crisis start? The year 2032, 2049, 2059, or 2047? I picked 2049, because it could be easily confused with two other answers.

A red check mark appeared, and Question Two replaced Question One. What caused the crisis? An asteroid, a volcanic eruption, an epidemic, or a biological agent? Since I knew the Wasteland had been caused by a man-made microbe that ate black topsoil and turned it into gray powder, I selected D. Another check mark.

Question Three: What country released the biological agent? NorAm, China, Turkey-Iran, or Egypt? I was fairly sure NorAm had been the victim, not the perpetrator, but I couldn't remember with whom NorAm had been at war at the time. I guessed Egypt, but an X appeared and Turkey-Iran became highlighted.

I got the next five questions right, remembering that the blight had soon spread over the whole globe and that the Earth would have become one huge wasteland if the United Nations hadn't developed an antibody that killed the microbe. Not that the UN had just handed the antibody out for free. Instead, they'd used their possession of the antibody as a way to stop traditional warfare. Countries had been forced to surrender all their weapons of mass destruction or be eaten by the blight.

Question Nine—What effect did the World Environmental Crisis have on mining?—stumped me for a moment. In the end I selected A, the UN began enforcing strict environmental laws, making mining on Earth more expensive. The wording "on Earth" made me remember that SilverDollar had a number of mines on Mars, where there was no environment to pollute.

That gave me a ninety percent, and I went on to

the next module on strip mining, about which I knew nothing. I was forced to yawn my way through twenty-five pages of dense information before I could pass the test.

As soon as it was suppertime, I went to the cafeteria. Anaximander always ate promptly at six, and I wanted to pump him for information regarding Michael Vallant.

Anaximander was very health-conscious so I loaded up my plate with vegetables and brown bread. I didn't want to waste time being lectured about my diet.

"So how did things go with the thief?" I asked, setting my tray down beside Anaximander's. Small talk was wasted on him. "Did he tell you where he hid the loot?"

"The interrogation was successful." Anaximander gave nothing away.

"So what happens to him now?" I asked casually. "Does he go to prison?" What would be my punishment if I had, in fact, been Michael Vallant's partner?

Anaximander surprised me. "No. In return for SilverDollar's dropping the charges he has agreed to work for us. After his Loyalty Induction, he'll join you in training."

My jaw dropped open. I closed it hastily, but long after supper was over and the pickup volleyball game in the gym had fizzled out, Anaximander's revelation kept exploding over and over in my mind.

I'd been hoping to make some friends my age at SilverDollar, but Michael Vallant wasn't whom I'd had in mind. Laying aside the problem of whether or not we knew each other, he was a thief. A criminal. How could I work with him?

But what disturbed me the most was the thought of Michael Vallant undergoing Loyalty Induction. Logically, I knew that Loyalty Induction was necessary to prevent industrial spies from infiltrating SilverDollar. I remembered my own Induction only vaguely, but I knew it had been rigorous, verging on painful. For some reason the thought of the violet-eyed thief experiencing even the small amount of pain caused by the Loyalty Induction bothered me—greatly.

Evenings at SilverDollar were always long—most of the other employees spent the time with their families, leaving me at loose ends—but this evening dragged on for years. I spent it rereading the articles I'd downloaded, searching for some clue I'd missed, and not finding anything. I was about to resort to watching *Escape from History* again when I came to my senses and went to bed early instead.

Black dreams woke me, in which I chased myself through the maze, never able to catch the Angel from the past to demand answers.

Cold, I rubbed my upper arms, trying to create some friction heat. My thumb traced the raised surface of a scar on my inner arm, following lines and curved shapes.

Letters.

"Computer, lights on." Heart pounding, I lifted my arm over my head. Twisting my head so far around made my neck ache, so I went into the bathroom for a better look. The jumble of lines resolved itself into letters, a word written in mirror writing, another message from Angel in the past.

A message so important I'd carved it in my own flesh.

"Michelangelo."

This message clearly referred to the second one I'd found, as Michelangelo had been a great Renaissance artist, but my mind saw a different, hidden meaning: Michael + Angel.

I shivered, icy with something I didn't understand, didn't remember.

Sleep was impossible. Driven by a need I couldn't deny, I dressed and slipped out the door. I had to see Michael Vallant.

My footsteps echoed down the deserted halls as I hurried from Blue to Gray Section. Two levels down in the subbasement, I stopped in front of the gunmetal gray door labeled L.I. for Loyalty Induction. The door was locked, but last week Anaximander had taught me how to jimmy card-locks and this one opened easily.

I eased open the door and, thankfully, found that the room beyond was empty. The technicians must have all returned to their quarters for the night. The large one-way window in the far wall drew my gaze. I stood with one hand pressed against the glass, looking in.

I'd forgotten the chamber's odd dimensions: two stories high but only eight feet square. The room was utterly bare. Its starkness chilled me, as if it were an old-fashioned prison cell where men were thrown after being tortured for information.

Michael Vallant sat leaning against the opposite wall. His dark hair was mussed, and there were bags under his eyes, but I couldn't take my eyes off him.

He was very deliberately staring at the one-way wall that hid the Observation Room, making a statement that he knew he was being watched. He was awake, and now I remembered why: sleep deprivation was part of the Loyalty Induction procedure. Hidden speakers inside the chamber produced an earsplitting screech that prowled up and down the limits of human hearing.

A video camera recorded everything that happened in the room; no doubt the technicians would fast forward through the tape in the morning to see how Michael Vallant had fared during the night.

I turned off the camera. If anything happened that the technicians needed to know about, I would tell them. If it was all foolishness on my part, I didn't want any witnesses.

As soon as I stepped inside, a high-pitched whine assaulted my ears, scraping my nerves raw.

Michael Vallant's head came up when he saw me, and he stood. "Finally." There was both relief and anger in his voice. "Get me out of here." He held out his bound hands.

I took a step back. "I can't do that." The sight of the padded handcuffs and chains he wore made me feel sick. I had to keeping reminding myself that Michael Vallant had agreed to the Loyalty Induction and the restraints were there to keep him from momentarily changing his mind about taking the oath.

"Then when?" Michael Vallant demanded. "The noise is driving me crazy." He didn't wait for me to answer. "Have you got the money yet?"

"What money?" I felt cold. He did know me. We had been partners. I was a criminal.

Michael didn't answer, staring. "Angel?"

A screech from the speakers made me flinch. "What money?" I asked.

"Angel, what's wrong?" Michael spoke without moving his lips, his expression urgent. "Is it Anaximander? Is he watching us? Tap your left foot if he is."

"No," I said aloud, lips moving, "I'm alone."

He stared at me a moment longer, then apparently took me at my word. "Then what's with you? Why didn't you warn me before you hit me with Knockout? I have bruises from the way I fell."

I started to back away. "I didn't warn you because I work for SilverDollar and you stole from them."

He stared, violet eyes intense. "What?"

"I don't know you. I never saw you before this afternoon."

He kept staring at me as if I was crazy. "What have they done to you?" he whispered.

I spoke faster, my skin crawling with the need to get out of the tiny chamber and its prickly shrieking. "I hit my head eleven days ago. I don't remember you. I don't *want* to remember you or anything criminal we might have done together. I don't care what the messages say. I don't know you."

I slammed out of the room, the door locking automatically behind me, walking fast, fleeing—then had to stop, go back, and turn the video camera on. I pretended I didn't hear Michael call my name in despair, "Angel!"

CHAPTER

5

THE NEXT DAY passed so slowly I thought I would lose my mind. Not even a flying lesson could hold my attention. After the second time Anaximander had to take over to prevent us from crashing, he flew us back to camp. I tensed in expectation of a lecture, but Anaximander just studied me for a moment and then sent me to study indoors.

I started to go to the doctor twice and to Anaximander a dozen times, but something always stopped me. Michael Vallant had behaved as if we were partners. If he was telling the truth, then I was a possible security risk if my memory returned and I should turn myself in. If he was lying, as the message "Violet eyes lie" said, then I wasn't a security risk—but if I hadn't known Michael Vallant before, then how could the message refer to him? I went round and round in circles all day.

In the back of my mind burned the knowledge that Michael Vallant's Loyalty Induction would be continuing all day, getting more and more intense.

It was a relief finally to reach the privacy of my own room after supper. I locked the door and feverishly began searching everything, including myself, for more messages from my past self.

It struck me as significant that two of the messages I'd found had been in the one outfit I owned that hadn't been bought for me by SilverDollar, so I concentrated on my purple sweater and blue jeans.

My hunch paid off. I found a scrap of paper tucked inside the unraveling hem of my purple sweater which said, "Dr. Frankenstein," and gave me another brief stab of recognition—*a fat man with glasses*—before stagnant green water closed over my head and the smell of the bog filled my nostrils once more.

The tiny flash of memory hardly seemed worth reliving the horror of drowning. I became angry at my past self. Why couldn't I have been more clear?

The next message was even less help. On the sole of my foot I found another mirror-writing scar, a date, or possibly a number, saying simply "1987."

I badly wanted to do another computer database search but didn't dare.

I searched the rest of my room, but if there were other messages I couldn't find them. There just weren't that many places to look. I didn't have very many personal possessions—no computer games, no e-books, no teddy bears, not even a clock—and for the first time I wondered why.

I smoothed back my rising panic by telling myself that I must be storing my possessions somewhere else, that I'd just forgotten where they were because of my head injury. I tried to believe it, but it seemed wrong that I wouldn't have brought something with me, a photo of my family, for instance.

My parents. I was suddenly gasping. Oh, God. I'd forgotten I had parents. Where were they? What did they look like? I couldn't remember.

For the first time I stopped thinking in terms of what I'd forgotten and tried to think of what I did remember about my past before coming to SilverDollar. The answer was a big fat nothing. I didn't remember my parents, didn't know if I had brothers and sisters or where I'd grown up.

A terrible thought occurred to me. Michael had known me in the past. He might know who my parents were. He could answer my questions.

I held out until one in the morning, when the halls were likely to be deserted, before I gave in and went to see Michael Vallant again. I had to know.

He didn't look surprised to see me; he looked as if he was in pain. He was slumped against the same wall as before, his violet eyes two deep wells burning in his ashen face.

The Loyalty Induction is causing him a lot more than discomfort.

It hurt me to see him suffering. I wanted to run to his side. Desperately, I reminded myself that he had consented to the Loyalty Induction just as I had.

Lines of pain bracketed his mouth.

I've kissed that mouth, I thought suddenly. The memory made me dizzy: *lying on my back beside a pool, dripping wet, my head tipped back at an awkward angle, warm lips covering mine . . .*

And then I was drowning. Again. Damn it.

"What do you want?" Michael asked when my head cleared.

I had no subtlety left. "Did you know my parents?"

He swallowed painfully. "Not really well, but yeah, I knew them."

"What are they like? Are they still alive?" I raised my voice above the screeching of the speakers; my fingernails dug into the soft flesh of my palms.

"Last time you saw them they were fine. There's no reason why they wouldn't be now," Michael said. "As for what they were like, I only met them a couple of times. You seemed to like them well enough."

Other questions boiled inside me: Where were my parents now? Why wasn't I in contact with them anymore? What did they look like? Were they blond like me? What did they do for a living? But it didn't sound as if Michael had the answers.

"So I'm not the only person you've forgotten, then?" Michael asked hoarsely.

"No." I twisted my lips into a smile. "You can laugh, but I was starting to be afraid that I didn't have parents at all, that I was just some genetic experiment mixed together in a petri dish." The fear that had been with me since viewing *Escape from History* drained away. "I have parents."

"You have adoptive parents," Michael corrected, plunging me back into uncertainty. "You and I are both genetically engineered."

"Project Renaissance?" I asked. My heart thumped in my chest.

He licked cracked lips. "Let's make a deal. I'll

tell you about Project Renaissance, if you answer my questions."

I couldn't make him tell me, and he was the best source of information I had. I nodded reluctant permission.

"The last time you visited me, you said I had stolen from SilverDollar. What is it I'm supposed to have stolen?"

"I don't know," I had to admit. "Something worth millions."

"I'm not a thief." Michael's violet eyes met mine. "Not unless it's possible to steal yourself. You and I are worth millions, but we belong to ourselves, not to a corporation."

He had to be lying, but I didn't argue the point. "Tell me about Project Renaissance."

He didn't try to cheat. "Project Renaissance is the code name for an illegal genetic experiment cooked up by NorAm twenty years ago. They successfully created a new subspecies of human, *Homo sapiens renascentia*. Renaissance, meaning the rebirth of humankind. They gave all the Renaissance children violet eyes as a genetic marker."

I felt sick. "So you and I belong to a different subspecies?" *Homo sapiens renascentia*, he'd said. Current humankind was *Homo sapiens sapiens*. Neanderthal man had been *Homo sapiens neanderthalensis*.

"Yes," Michael said. "My turn. If you've forgotten your past, how did you know about Project Renaissance?"

I hesitated, then explained about the hidden messages that I didn't remember writing pricked into torn-up paper. "There's also a scar on my arm that says 'Michelangelo.' What does it mean?"

"What you think it means. Michael and Angel."

"And?"

"It's a code name," he said hoarsely. "Dr. Frankenstein gave it to us. When Project Renaissance was discovered there was a big scandal. The UN stopped the project, but they didn't know what to do with the violet-eyed children that had already been created. We were put in an orphanage, but some fanatics burned it down. The survivors were paired up and put into different Historical Immersion towns."

"You mean that stupid movie was true?" I was appalled.

"*Escape from History?*" Michael snorted. "No, it's not true, except for the general outline. We killed ourselves laughing watching the movie when it came out a couple of months ago. They got almost everything wrong."

"What did they get right?" I asked.

"Other than the fact that we were raised as if we were living a hundred years in the past, not much. They got the cameras right. We lived under constant surveillance. Dr. Frankenstein studied us as if we were lab rats."

"Why?" I asked. "So we're smart. Big deal."

"It's not just intelligence," Michael said. "It's the whole package. In addition to being smarter than *sapiens*, we're also world-class athletes and have faster reflexes. We're healthier, too, with better immune systems. We were bred to be spies and assassins. We're a very valuable commodity. Why do you think SilverDollar is so eager to have us work for them?"

"I was hired as a security investigator. SilverDollar is a mining company, not a government," I said skeptically. "What do they need spies for?"

"I don't know exactly," Michael admitted. "Probably industrial espionage. Infiltrating a rival company, stealing their secrets, maybe committing acts of sabotage . . . SilverDollar tried to buy us from Dr. Frankenstein, and when we escaped, they hunted us down as if we were foxes. Anaximander and his men have been pursuing us relentlessly since we escaped five months ago, in November. They must have some need for us."

"That can't be true," I said. "Companies can't just go around buying people or kidnapping them off the street. Why didn't we just go to the police?"

"And put ourselves back in the hands of the government that failed us twice before?" Michael asked. "No thank you. Besides, some would say you and I aren't 'people.' We were genetic experiments, remember? Property. Don't you get it? We're different, Angel. The prejudice the Augmented face is nothing compared to the hostility leveled at the violet-eyed. Ordinary people look at us, and they see a threat. Unfair competition in the job market and the gene pool. They're afraid that, if we're left to ourselves, in a few generations Renaissance children will become the de facto rulers of the world and they'll be the serving class."

"That's crazy," I said.

"You and I know that," Michael said wearily. "They don't. That's why SilverDollar could pursue us without worrying about the law. They knew we didn't dare risk our cover. We stayed one step ahead of Anaximander, but it was costing us. We could never stay in one place long enough to save any money or make any friends."

"What did we do?" I asked.

"We haunted the library, learning as much as we could about the new time we found ourselves in, and we earned money doing menial labor: shoveling snow, dishwashing, baby-sitting, that sort of thing. A better job would have required ID, which we don't have. In 2099 you need ID to do everything: get a library card, fly an aircar, get an education.

"We lived like that for five months, barely surviving. Toward the end, we were tired all the time and twitchy from living in constant fear of discovery. Finally, we decided to let Anaximander capture one of us. That person would try to obtain identicards and money from the inside."

"Steal, you mean," I said bitterly. He was a thief.

"Compensation," Michael argued. "Reparation. They've been persecuting us, trying to kidnap and enslave us. It looks to me as if they've succeeded with you."

"I'm not a slave," I said at once.

"They've brainwashed you, the same as they're trying to brainwash me. They installed a Loyalty chip in your head and erased your memory." Michael's gaze was intense.

"I don't have a Loyalty chip."

"Oh, come on," Michael scoffed. "There's still a bandage on your head from the surgery."

My hand went automatically to my forehead. I'd heard of Loyalty chips; they were evil inventions. SilverDollar would never use one. "This is from a training accident."

"Are you sure?" Michael asked. "Do you remember it?"

I tried once more to remember falling from a rope. Heard again the hesitation in Anaximander's voice before he answered my question. . . . "That's not unusual with head injuries," I said defensively.

Michael nodded, as if I'd admitted something. "They've brainwashed you, and now they're going to brainwash me. You have to help me, Angel. Let me out of here."

"I don't believe you," I said, but nausea churned inside me because I wasn't sure.

"Prove SilverDollar is innocent. Look under the bandage."

I didn't want to, and Michael read that in my face. My chin went up. I tore off the bandage.

I don't know what I expected—flashing computer lights, maybe—but all my fingers felt was a three-inch cut, neatly sewn up. No Loyalty chip.

"The incision is on the frontal lobe where Loyalty chips are installed," Michael said.

I stopped breathing, then saw the pleased smile touching his lips. "You made that up."

He didn't deny it.

I was disgusted with myself. "My own note warned me not to trust you. 'Violet eyes lie.' "

Michael looked puzzled for a moment, then his eyes widened.

"You know what it means," I accused.

"You were telling yourself to lie in order to gain your freedom," Michael said smoothly.

I didn't believe him. I couldn't tell if anything he'd told me was the truth. "How do I know you aren't one of the bad guys, like Judas in the movie?"

"Who?" Michael looked confused for a moment. "Oh, right. The guy who got the blonde pregnant. That part wasn't us, that was Vincent Cole and Erin Reinders. Never mind that. I am not Judas."

The names Vincent Cole and Erin Reinders triggered the drowning memory again. "Who are Vincent and Erin?" I asked quickly when I resurfaced, trying to distract Michael from my pallor.

"Vincent and his sister, Leona, are two other Renaissance children we met. They were being blackmailed into helping Dr. Frankenstein. Vincent had gotten Erin Reinders pregnant, and Dr. Frankenstein was holding the baby's fate over their heads. They escaped at the same time we did."

I had no memory of the event, but I was inclined to believe Michael this time. Somehow the story rang true. "How did we escape?"

Michael's expression became remote. "Dr. Frankenstein was crazy. He challenged us to a duel to the death, to prove who was smarter, *sapiens* or *renascentia*. He lost."

"He's dead?"

"Yes."

That was all Michael said, but I shivered.

"Come on, Angel," Michael coaxed. "Say you remember me."

I bit my lip. I didn't. Not really.

During our conversation, I'd come dangerously close to Michael. He reached out with his cuffed hands and touched the gold chain around my throat. "You're still wearing it. The angel pendant I gave you at Christmas. You must remember me." Hope and exultation in his voice.

I shook my head and stepped back, but my

fingers cradled the pendant protectively. "No. I'm sorry."

The disappointment in his face pierced me, and I quickly asked him another question. "The number 1987. What does it mean?"

His lips quirked. "Ah, how romantic. Nineteen eighty-seven is the year we met."

Today was April 19, 2099. Neither of us had been born in 1987, so the Historical Immersion towns where we'd been raised must have been set in 1987. I wasn't learning anything new.

"This is a waste of time," I said abruptly. "I'm leaving."

"No!" Real panic showed on Michael Vallant's face. He grabbed my wrist. "You can't leave me like this! Tomorrow they'll wipe away my memory and install a Loyalty chip in me. You have to help me."

Frightened, I broke his grip and backed away.

"If you won't listen to me, listen to yourself," Michael called after me. "You left another message here in the brainwash chamber. It's up there on the wall." He pointed with his bound hands.

I eyed him suspiciously in case it was a trap, but in the end I couldn't fight the compulsion to look. The bare concrete wall had scratches in it, invisible from more than half a foot away. I recognized my handwriting.

"Mike, if you find yourself here, it's because I betrayed you. I'm so sorry. It gets harder to fight every day."

My blood ran cold. I staggered as the drowning memory sucked at me, but when it was over the message was still there. "It can't be true," I whispered. "SilverDollar wouldn't do that."

"You only think so because your Loyalty chip is making you think so," Mike said.

I shook my head, mute.

"Keep reading," Mike said.

"Anaximander came to see me today. He almost looked worried. He said people have died from resisting Loyalty Induction, their minds rebounding in on themselves. They put the chip in tomorrow."

I looked to Mike.

"Let me go." His eyes entreated mine.

I took a step forward. Stopped. "I can't."

We stared at each other for several minutes, before Mike's expression changed into one of weary resignation. "Your Loyalty chip won't let you release me."

I opened my mouth but couldn't refute his words.

"It's okay," Mike said, eerily calm. "Go back to your room. I forgive you."

Thoughts in turmoil, I backed out of the chamber. In the hall, I leaned against the wall, my body bowed in anguish. I couldn't bear the thought of Mike being cut open tomorrow and his will taken away. It was wrong.

Wrong. I clung to the word, studied it from all sides, found a chink.

Loyalty chips were wrong. I was certain SilverDollar wouldn't do something both immoral and illegal, therefore an overzealous employee must be responsible. Since SilverDollar could get into a lot of trouble if they were discovered using Loyalty chips, it was my duty as a loyal employee to keep the company from unknowingly perpetrating an illegal act.

There was a huge flaw in my thinking somewhere, but I let it go, didn't think about it. I turned
off the video camera and went back inside.

Mike's eyes were shut against the horrible
whine coming from the speakers. When he opened
them and saw me, he looked astonished.

I quickly explained my reasoning, while unlock-
ing his cuffs with a key I'd found in the
Observation Room. "SilverDollar wouldn't do this,
I know it."

"Oh, yes, SilverDollar would," Mike said grimly,
rubbing his wrists.

"We don't have time to argue," I said. "Follow
me."

Mike stopped suddenly, halfway across the
chamber. He stooped and picked something small
off the floor.

"What is it?" I asked.

He smiled, and his whole face lit up. "A paper
clip." He opened his hands and showed me. It was,
indeed, a paper clip, bent open and crooked. One
end looked rusty.

"So?"

"So this is how you wrote your messages." Mike
laughed, and my breath caught in my throat. He
was gorgeous when he laughed. "They didn't
search you for messages because they didn't think
you had a means of writing anything. You beat
them with a paper clip and an old receipt. God, I
love you, Angel. A paper clip." He laughed again.

I stood still, overwhelmed by a memory and the
drowning that immediately followed. But this time
I kept the memory. *Mike handing me a small, slim
box at Christmastime. Opening it and seeing the*

necklace glittering within. And crying. Crying, because although the angel was beautiful, it wasn't what I'd wanted for Christmas.

I'd wanted the words. Even though I'd known how Mike felt about me, I'd wanted the words.

And now my heart shattered over finally hearing him say "I love you"—

—and not being able to say the words back.

"What is it?" Mike asked.

I shook my head, mute and angry. I didn't have time for a trip down memory lane right now, and it didn't matter what Mike's feelings for me were. "Hurry," I said.

It took us twenty minutes to reach an exit; Mike walked as if he were an old man, weakened by his ordeal. "Here." I opened a small side door in Blue Section, revealing the starry night outside. "Go. I'll find out who's responsible, I swear."

Mike halted. "Aren't you coming?"

I blinked, astonished. The thought had not crossed my mind.

"Angel, you have to come," Mike said urgently. "The Loyalty chip is affecting your thinking. Come with me, and we'll dismantle it somehow."

I was shaking my head. "I belong here." I could see him weighing his chances of knocking me out and taking me away by force. "Don't try it," I warned.

"I'm not leaving without you."

His words filled me with an odd kind of panic. *He had to leave.* Panic made me brutal. "Go. I may have known you once, but I don't now. You're a stranger to me."

"No." He shook his head, swaying on his feet. "I'm not going."

"Why not?" I was near tears. It would be so much simpler if he left.

Mike favored me with a twisted smile. "Because you would never leave me. You came back for me once when you shouldn't have, when you knew Dr. Frankenstein was setting a trap." Softly, "I failed you once. I won't do it again."

CHAPTER

6

I STARED AT MIKE in frustration. "Are you crazy? You have to leave."

"No. Not without you."

He meant it, I realized with a shock. He wasn't leaving. I fought the warm glow that wanted to spread through me. "If you stay, they'll install the Loyalty chip in your head."

His gaze remained steady. "Not if you help me."

I wanted to, but I wasn't sure that I could.

"All you have to do is find the Loyalty chip they plan to install tomorrow and sabotage it," Mike said.

"Oh, is that all?" I asked sarcastically. "What if I can't find it? Even if I do, it won't help because I don't know how to disable a Loyalty chip."

"I trust you," Mike said. "I'll risk it."

I stared at him, appalled. How could he trust me? I was the one who had captured him, betrayed him, and the chip in my head would make me do the same thing again.

Without another word, we headed back, Mike's arm draped over my shoulders for support.

"I don't know how much discrepancy on the videotape we can get away with before the technicians notice," I said, planning ahead. "You'll have to go back in the chamber and rechain yourself while I search for the chip. Position yourself as closely as you can to where you were when I came in."

"No problem." When we reached the Loyalty Induction chamber, Mike went inside without a word of advice or caution. *He trusted me*. The thought made me dizzy.

Determined not to let him down, I searched the Observation Room thoroughly. I found a supply of medi-patches: Knockout and TrueFalse, and others I didn't recognize.

A second gray door opened off the Observation Room to the left. Inside, I found a stainless steel surgery. It made me queasy to think about Mike's skull being cut open tomorrow. Would Dr. Clark perform the operation, or was it a matter for an engineer? Had I lain on that cold table? I shivered.

I found the Loyalty chip inside a locked cupboard. At least, I thought it was the Loyalty chip: a wafer-thin black object the size of my fingernail with clusters of cilia-like fibers growing out of it. Neural connectors?

I wanted to grind the hateful thing under my foot, but that would only delay Mike's brainwashing while they got a replacement chip, not stop it.

Viciously deciding that Mike was crazy to trust me, I pried open the Loyalty chip along its hair-thin seam. An even tinier circuit board winked inside. I thought about scoring the delicate lines etched on the silicon with my fingernail, but hesitated. What if all I did was damage the chip, and when it was installed Mike's brain got fried? I was nearing despair—Mike would just have to leave without me, that was all—when I hit upon the obvious.

The chip itself wasn't dangerous to Mike; the connections between Mike's brain and the chip were what allowed it to interface with him. All I had to do was disconnect the chip from the neural connectors.

Fingers clumsy with haste, I ripped the chip out of its nest inside the black casing. Once I'd satisfied myself there were no connections left, I put the chip back inside and snapped the halves of the black casing back together, taking care not to catch any of the cilia inside. It looked the same to me as it had before I'd opened it. I replaced it on its shelf and relocked the cupboard.

After turning on the video camera again, I told Mike what I'd done, trying to be positive. "As long as the chip was already programmed and all they plan to do is install it tomorrow morning, they shouldn't notice the sabotage. If you can fake your way through whatever testing procedures they try on the chip, you should be fine." My stomach did a slow roll at the thought.

"It'll work," Mike said intensely. "But if it doesn't, promise me that you'll do the same for me that you did for yourself with the paper clip." His cuffed hands framed my face. "Promise me that you'll tell me who I am. That you won't let me forget."

"I promise." I turned toward the door before Mike could see my tears and the lie in my eyes. How could I help Mike when I remembered only the barest part of who he was? And if the chip's sabotage was discovered, my part in it likely would be, too, and I'd find myself back in the Loyalty chamber with him.

I slipped out into the hall. It was close to five in the morning, and there was no one around.

I wanted quite badly to set a watch on the door to the Loyalty Induction room, to see who was going to install Mike's chip, but I would be too obvious, loitering in the hallway. So I went back to my quarters and lay down but didn't manage to sleep.

All too soon it was time to get up again. I stumbled through a five-mile run with Anaximander in a haze, suspense sawing at my nerves. I lived through terrible scenarios of something going wrong with the Loyalty chip because of my oh-so-clever fiddling, and Mike turning into a vegetable.

Whoever Mike was to me, I didn't want him dead.

"No computer lessons this morning," Anaximander said when we'd finished. "You're to write a fifteen-hundred-word essay instead. The topic is: 'The Future of Mars.' Be finished by noon."

Essay writing had nothing to do with my job description, but my wits were too dulled to protest. As soon as Anaximander left, I returned to my bedroom and napped. At 10:30 A.M, I woke and wrote the essay in furious haste, churning out fourteen hundred words by 12:15 P.M. Mars turned out to be an interesting topic. In my essay, I advocated "terraforming" Mars—making its atmosphere and ecology more Earthlike so humans could live on it without domes—since I found the most information on that subject.

I added another hundred words during lunch hour and was revising the last sentence when Anaximander found me at 1:00 P.M.

Eddy came with him. "Hello, Angel. Have you been angelic?" He laughed at his little joke.

My boss, the comedian. I lacked the energy to dredge up a smile, so I just handed Anaximander a disk with my essay on it. "Why did you want me to write an essay on Mars?"

Eddy answered. "You're entering a contest."

Obviously, I hadn't had enough sleep, because I didn't understand. "What?"

"Once your training is finished, I'm thinking of sending you to Mars on assignment. So I want you to attend a student symposium on the future of Mars to give you some background. My nephew, Timothy, is running the show. SilverDollar is sponsoring it. There will be a bunch of lectures about Mars, and there's a contest."

"What's the prize?" I asked, curious.

"A trip to Mars or seventy-five thousand dollars' cash. Timothy's idea. He's crazy about Mars, a real Martian! So how does attending the symposium strike you?"

"Sounds like fun. When does it start?" My tiredness began to leave me. The symposium would give me a chance to get out of dull SilverDollar and meet people my age.

"You fly out this afternoon," Eddy said, his words like a splash of cold water.

This afternoon. If I left this afternoon, I wouldn't have a chance to check on Mike. I wouldn't know if I'd succeeded in breaking his Loyalty chip or if I'd killed him.

I hung onto my smile by the skin of my teeth. "Great!"

Eddy didn't notice the falseness in my voice. "Anaximander's running security for the event, and I'm one of the contest judges. Perhaps the next time I see you, I'll be presenting the award to you!"

My smile began to feel as if it were fixed in cement.

"Anaximander, why don't you wait outside while I speak to Angel alone for a moment?" Eddy flashed a predatory smile.

Anaximander didn't move. "What do you want to discuss?"

Eddy opened his suit jacket and began to play with the black butterfly token. Anaximander's gaze was drawn to it as if to a lodestone. "I said, leave us."

Anaximander shook his head as if to clear away cobwebs. "Yes, sir." He walked slowly toward the door, his body language reluctant. I had the odd impression that Anaximander wanted to protect me.

I gave a slight nod when Anaximander stopped and looked at me. I would be fine. Eddy was a creep, but I could handle him.

And then a very odd thing happened. Anaximander, whose Augments gave him better than 20/20 vision, missed the door and walked into a wall.

He didn't just graze the wall; he walked full into

it. It must have hurt, but he just tried again and walked out the door.

Eddy slapped his knee, laughing. "Did you see that? Did you see what the big robot did?"

Robot was the worst insult one could make to the Augmented. I stiffened on Anaximander's behalf.

"Oh, don't look so mad. Loosen up. It was just a little joke." Eddy punched my shoulder.

"It wasn't funny." I resisted the urge to punch him back.

Eddy's expression turned mean. "I thought it was."

A hard silence fell, and then I blinked, and when I next looked, Eddy had relaxed. He smiled slyly, as if he knew a secret I did not. "I want to talk to you about Timothy."

I waited.

"The truth is, I'm a little worried about Timothy. I'd like you to keep an eye on him while you're at the symposium. You're the same age as Timothy, eighteen. I want you to befriend him. Cheer him up if he gets depressed."

My enthusiasm for the trip dimmed. It sounded like Eddy wanted me to be a baby-sitter. "Does he get depressed often?" I asked. "I mean, did his dog die or something?"

Eddy ignored my questions. "Now, the thing is, I don't want Timothy to know that you work for me—he'll think I'm checking up on him."

And aren't you? I wondered.

"Just pretend to be another Martian," Eddy advised.

"Mars is cool," I said.

"Great." Eddy clapped me on the shoulder.

"Anaximander will brief you on the details. See you at the symposium."

As I watched him breeze out, I was bewildered to discover that my fists were clenched so hard it took actual effort to open them.

I gave Eddy thirty seconds' head start, then made for the door. I had to find out how Mike was. But when I opened the door, Anaximander was on the other side.

"You're not ready for a solo flight yet," he said, "so I'm having one of my men fly you out to Arizona in forty minutes."

Forty minutes didn't give me much time. I fought down my agitation. "So what is it that Eddy's not telling me? Why does Eddy's nephew rate his own symposium? What's my future assignment on Mars?"

"Timothy isn't just Mr. Castellan's nephew. He's also the son of SilverDollar's president," Anaximander said softly.

So Timothy was rich. I hoped he wasn't spoiled, too. "And Eddy is . . . ?" I asked.

"Madam President's half brother."

Well, that explained the creep's high office. "And the Mars assignment?" I asked.

"Mr. Castellan hasn't informed me what your assignment will be."

I narrowed my eyes. Not being told wasn't the same thing as not knowing. "Is there trouble with the Martian mines?"

"Who told you that?" Anaximander snapped.

"No one." I was taken aback by his reaction. "I was just guessing."

"It's a vicious rumor that just because the cost

of operating in space is getting higher, SilverDollar
will close the mines and put thousands of Spacers
out of work. Let me tell you something about the
Spacers before you start spreading rumors about
closing down their livelihood." Anaximander actually looked angry. My careless words had obviously hit a nerve; Anaximander must have had
some Spacer friends.

"The Spacers are a displaced people. The Blight
in 2049 left hundreds of thousands of people
crowded into refugee camps. In a desperate
attempt to stimulate the faltering world economy,
the UN began the monumental task of building a
beanstalk from Earth into space. The refugees
could have sat in the camps and moldered, waiting
for a cure for the Blight to be found, but some of
them petitioned the UN to be allowed to do something useful, to work on the beanstalk. They
started off as unskilled labor and got the worst
jobs and the lowest pay.

"Most went back to their homelands afterward,
but about twelve thousand decided to stay on and
adopt space as their new homeland. They and
their children became the Spacers. Three-quarters
of them work for SilverDollar's Mars operation. If
the mines on Mars shut down, they lose their
homeland again and a whole culture dies."

"I had no idea," I said.

"The cost of operating in space might be getting
higher," Anaximander said, "but it's the Spacers
who've had to pay the steepest price."

"Paid how?" I asked.

"In birth defects. Most Spacers are born need-
ing some sort of Augment."

I nodded, enlightened. The research I'd done on terraforming Mars had mentioned it in passing. The human body had been designed to live under Earth's gravity and did not take to the lighter gravities and zero-Gs of space. Coupled with a radiation problem from the lack of a Martian ozone layer and proper shielding of early Spacer domes, and it was no wonder the Spacers were prone to birth defects.

"SilverDollar has to pay for the high cost of Augmentation," Anaximander said. "But it's the Spacers who have to live with the Augments."

For the first time I wondered if Anaximander minded being Augmented. I'd somehow presumed that his titanium legs, Memory Recorder, Ear-radio, and silver eyes were all upgrades he'd had done to himself in a quest for perfection. It had never occurred to me that the Augments had been forced on him by a disability.

I tried to think of a way to express my sympathy, but the moment was lost when Anaximander handed me a palmtop computer, all business once more. "Here, this is yours. I've downloaded the itinerary for the symposium onto it."

The palmtop was bigger than my palm, but not by much, about six inches square. It was pretty small for something that was a TV, a vidphone, and a computer rolled into one. Its black leather carrying case had a strap that could be used to sling the palmtop diagonally across one's body.

"I don't know if Eddy plans to bring you back here after the symposium or send you straight on to your first assignment, so I might as well give you your supplies now." Anaximander led the way down the hall to a supply room and kitted me out with Knockout medi-patches, TrueFalse medi-patches, handcuffs, and a sticky-gag.

And another item I didn't recognize, a tiny atomizer. "What's this? Perfume?" I pretended to spray my neck.

Anaximander plucked it out of my hand and packed it in its case. "It's your insurance. If you get hit with a Knockout patch, you have ten seconds to inhale this spray. It will hyperoxygenate your blood to prevent you from passing out."

"Cool. Body armor for Knockout patches."

"Except that regular body armor doesn't dissolve fifteen minutes later, leaving you unprotected," Anaximander said dryly. "Hyperoxygenation wears off quickly. That's everything. You're set." Anaximander paused awkwardly. "Angel—"

"You don't have to say it," I told him. "I'm well aware that you don't think I'm ready to go on a solo assignment."

"No, I don't," Anaximander said bluntly.

I winced inside. I'd been hoping he would correct me.

"If I were in charge I would never have hired you. I think you're too young for what the job requires." Anaximander paused. "Which is why I've been so hard on you. I kept hoping you'd back down and realize you were in over your head. But you never did."

I perked up a little. That had sounded suspiciously like a compliment.

"It's not your skills that I doubt, Angel. You're fast, and you think on your feet better than anyone I've ever known. It's your toughness that I worry about. Some of the tasks I've done for Mr. Castellan have been . . . unpleasant."

I stopped on the verge of assuring Anaximander that I was tough. What exactly did he mean by "unpleasant"? Unwillingly, I remembered Mike's speculation that SilverDollar had hired us to do industrial espionage.

But Anaximander was through being forthcoming. "Your aircar leaves in twenty minutes. You'd better get going."

I left the room at a sedate walk but was running when I turned the first corner. I headed for the subbasement in Gray Section, the Knockout patches Anaximander had just given me in hand. I *had* to see Mike before I left.

Someone was coming down the hall, so I twisted the doorknob to the Loyalty Induction room as if I had every right to go in. I planned to put on a show of searching my pockets for a nonexistent cardkey, but the door wasn't locked. I slipped inside.

The Observation Room was empty. So was the Loyalty Induction chamber on the other side of the window.

I listened at the door to the surgery, then opened it, too.

A heavy antiseptic smell hung in the air, but Mike was gone. And I was out of time. I left Taber not knowing if he was okay. Or insane. Or dead.

CHAPTER

IN THE PASSENGER SEAT of the aircar I stared at my new identicard with deep unease.

The picture was of me. The birth date was mine. My name was even spelled correctly, Angel Eastland.

So why was I upset?

I heard Mike's voice in my mind: "In 2099 you need ID to do everything. . . . Finally, we decided to let Anaximander capture one of us. That person would try to obtain identicards and money from the inside."

I now had half of what Mike and the Angel he'd known had risked so much to get.

So what? I asked myself sternly. *That was the old Angel. The new Angel isn't on the run, and she's the one with the card.*

Sometimes I felt as if there were two Angels, Shadow Angel and New Angel. Shadow Angel was hiding somewhere inside me. Sometimes I caught echoes of her voice, but that was all.

I hated the way Shadow Angel kept manipulating me, but if I lost her I was deathly afraid I would lose myself.

Shadow Angel. New Angel. For a moment I felt as if I were fracturing inside. Frightened, I fought down the feeling and looked out the windows of the aircar instead.

The pilot landed me at the SilverDollar Tucson facility, and I registered for the symposium.

To give me a leg up in making friends with his nephew, Eddy had arranged for me to be billeted with the Castellan family. I sent my luggage ahead, but chose to walk myself to get a feel for the place. The warm desert sun felt good on my back.

Unlike the Taber building, SilverDollar Tucson had scorned the glossy, high-tech look in favor of charming haciendas with red-tiled roofs. The motorized walkways that connected the complex were below ground, their presence advertised only by discreet gold-plate markers. The lawns that I walked through had been irrigated green, and the trees were old and mighty (if they were force-grown I couldn't tell.)

Two orange trees marked the Castellan house. It was large but not the mansion I'd expected.

A middle-aged woman in a vivid pink dress answered the door. Her walnut brown hair was coiled neatly at the nape of her neck. "You are Miss Angel?" She had a Spanish accent.

I nodded.

"I am Graciana Pasos, the housekeeper. Con–gratulations."

"On what?" I asked, startled.

"Were you not told? You are a finalist in Mr. Timothy's contest."

"That's good news," I lied. How could I be a finalist? I'd only just written the essay, and I'd written it in frantic haste.

The answer was simple. I couldn't be a finalist in a legitimate contest. Eddy must have cheated to have my name added to the list. But why? "Are all the finalists staying here in this house?" I asked.

"Yes." She motioned me inside and I followed. "Mr. Timothy apologizes for not being here to meet you. There is a message for you in the living room." She showed me the vidphone, then withdrew.

From Graciana's wording, I had expected the recording to be from Timothy, so I was jolted when a video image of a silver-haired woman in a cherry red suit came up.

I didn't recognize her; I hoped she wasn't someone I'd forgotten. My heart rate doubled. Could the message be from my mother? There were a dozen reasons why that was unlikely, but I was still bitterly disappointed when the woman's first words proved it.

"Ms. Eastland, I recognized your name when Timothy told me who the finalists were. I know you work for SilverDollar, which means you work for me."

This was *Timothy's* mother, I realized, president of SilverDollar. Which explained the large desk she was sitting behind.

She leaned forward so that her face filled the screen, and I could see the power radiating from her as well as the crow's feet in the corners of her eyes. "I assume Edward has planted you in the house to prevent a second kidnapping."

Kidnapping? A *second* kidnapping? There'd already been a first? Of whom?

"I thought about having you kicked out," President Castellan continued, "but Timothy would have to be told, and I don't want him upset right now. I'm going to let you stay, but understand this: you work for me, not Edward. If you do something I don't like, you will develop a terrible case of the flu and have to be flown home." Threat over, she sat back again. "Ms. Eastland, my son doesn't need a bodyguard. He needs a friend."

Click. The recording ended, leaving me with plenty of food for thought. And anger at Eddy. Why hadn't he, or Anaximander, mentioned that Timothy had once been kidnapped?

President Castellan didn't seem to like Eddy very much—had calling him by his full name been some sort of insult?—but reading between the lines, I could tell she was also worried about her son. Interesting.

Graciana erased the message, then gave me a quick tour of the house—kitchen, dining room, living room, a bathroom, and three bedrooms on the main floor; two more bedrooms, a second bathroom, and an office on the second floor. "Let me know if you need anything. Breakfast is at eight, supper is at six." Having delivered me to one of the main-floor bedrooms, she backed away.

The room I'd been given was much nicer than my SilverDollar one, with teal green wallpaper and two obviously brand-new twin beds with chintz

comforters, but I barely glanced at it. My roommate had arrived ahead of me.

She was black-skinned and tiny, so petite she
looked as if she ought to have fairy wings and be
able to fly. Except that this fairy princess couldn't
walk. Her legs were withered, and she sat in a
wheelchair.

In this day of Augments, wheelchairs were so
rare as to be almost nonexistent. Only the poor
still used wheelchairs.

Her clothes were strictly mall fare, a simple
orange T-shirt and blue jeans. Her hair was black
and kinky-curly, even within the tight confines of
several million braids. The braids were drawn up
into a short ponytail.

Her eyes were angry. They spat fire, looking me
up and down disdainfully.

I confused her by smiling. I was so happy to
have a roommate my age to talk to that I would
have smiled at Lizzie Borden. I tossed my bag on
the unoccupied bed. "Sorry. I was trying to decide
if it was more rude to ask what happened to your
legs or to pretend that I hadn't noticed you
couldn't walk."

She wasn't charmed. "Let me know when you
decide."

I walked over to her and held out my hand. "I'm
Angel Eastland. I don't snore."

"I'm Rianne Beaulieu. I do."

I laughed, and after a few seconds, Rianne per-
mitted herself a quick smile.

"So," I said, "should we be good and unpack or
goof off?"

Her reserve slammed right back into place.

"You can do whatever you want. I'm going to finish unpacking."

"Unpack it is," I said good-naturedly. "First one done gets to pick which bed she wants." Since Rianne was already halfway finished, I didn't feel guilty about opening up my suitcase and dumping its contents into a set of drawers.

As soon as Rianne saw what I was doing, she stopped neatly transferring items from her suitcase and started tossing them in with wild abandon.

I finished first, stuffing a dangling sleeve into the bulging drawer and shoving it closed. "There," I said brightly. "All done."

"So which bed do you want?" Rianne eyed me as if she couldn't decide whether I was crazy or fun.

"I don't know. I'll have to test them." I sat down on the left-hand one. "Hmmm. This mattress has nice firm edges. Good bounce." I tested each bed out thoroughly, going so far as to measure them for length even though it was obvious the beds were identical. I succeeded in making Rianne laugh and eventually settled for the bed closer to the door.

It felt good to make friends. I'd missed—

Who? Somebody.

Rianne had said something, but I didn't know what. "Let's go see what's on the menu for supper." I bounced to my feet.

In the living room we found two new arrivals. Graciana introduced them as Zinnia and Dahlia Cartwright.

Zinnia had chin-length white-blond hair. I

started when I saw that Zinnia's eyes were purple—was she one of the Renaissance children?—
but then I saw that her eyes matched her purple
silk blouse and that her lipstick and nails were also
the same shade.

She had to be wearing colored contacts, because
Dahlia had turquoise eyes and she was Zinnia's
identical twin. It took me a moment to realize their
features were the same since they were dressed so
differently. Zinnia had a cool classic style, while
Dahlia looked outrageous and funky in a peacock-
print jumpsuit and short blue hair.

The two of them made me feel quite drab in my
black shirt and pants. The clothing SilverDollar
had bought for me was so basic as to be fashion-
less, but they were supposed to have my body form
on record somewhere. I resolved to order some
new clothes soon.

"I want to trade rooms with one of you," the
outrageous one, Dahlia, said. She glared at her sister. "I don't want to stay with *her.*"

"It's not like I asked to share a room with you,"
Zinnia shot back. "The trustees should have made
it clear that we needed separate rooms when they
registered us," she told Graciana, who looked
upset.

"Trustees?" I asked.

They ignored me. "Will you trade?" Zinnia asked.

"I'm quite happy where I am," I stalled.

They both turned their attention on Rianne,
two heads swiveling in unison. The movement was
eerie. An Augment? I wondered, or just a twin
thing?

"Forget it," Rianne said. "I was here first."

Not to mention that her wheelchair couldn't go up stairs easily.

"Isn't there another room?" Zinnia asked.

Graciana shook her head. "The upstairs suite is Madam President's. The other two downstairs rooms are for boys—Mr. Timothy and another finalist."

"So?" Dahlia demanded. She seemed pushier than her twin was as well as more outrageous. "I'd rather bunk with a boy than *her*."

Graciana put her foot down. "No. No boys and girls sleeping together in this house."

Dahlia rolled her eyes. "As if I'd want to make out with some boy I've never met."

"Nevertheless," Graciana said serenely. "That is the rule. Supper will be ready in five minutes." She returned to the kitchen.

"You've *got* to trade with me," Dahlia said dramatically.

"Do either of you snore?" I asked.

"She does," they both said simultaneously.

I crossed my arms. "Then I think I'll stay right where I am."

Rianne's lips twitched.

Supper was a red beans and rice dish, tasty but spoiled somewhat by the Flower Twins' sniping. I finally discovered the reason behind their enmity when I referred to Zinnia as "your sister" while talking to Dahlia.

"She's not my sister! She's my clone!"

"I am not *your* clone!" Zinnia looked down her nose at Dahlia. "We're both Iris's clones."

"And who is Iris?" I asked when no one else did.

"Iris Cartwright," Zinnia said.

I looked blank.

"Oh, come on! Everyone knows who Iris Cartwright is," Dahlia said impatiently.

Graciana broke in quietly. "Iris Cartwright stopped the Blight. She was a hero."

"Oh, *that* Iris Cartwright," I said. Inside my heart was hammering. Another missing memory? "I thought cloning was illegal."

"It is," Zinnia said. "But our progenitor received special permission from the UN."

Special permission, I wondered, *or blackmail? Let me clone myself or I won't give you the cure for the Blight?*

"She knew that when she died her work reversing the Blight would be unfinished and that no one else had the genius to continue it. So she made us to carry forward her life's work."

Zinnia sounded awed, as if she was talking about some holy crusade, but to me it sounded creepy. Born just to carry on someone else's life as if she were some miserable shadow-thing?

"So that *one of us* can inherit her company and carry forward her life's work," Dahlia corrected. "And that someone is going to be me."

Anger and something else—sadness?—flashed across Zinnia's face before she picked up her fork again. "We'll find out when we graduate in June."

I suddenly understood why Iris Cartwright had made two clones instead of one. She wanted two in case one of the clones proved to have its own personality instead of being an exact copy.

Back in our room afterward, Rianne started laughing for no reason.

"What?" I asked.

"The look on their faces when you pretended not to know who Iris Cartwright was. One hundred percent priceless. I like you, Angel." Her wheelchair made her too short to punch my shoulder, so she thumped my knee instead.

I smirked back at her. "Glad you liked it." But it was all an act. I still didn't really know who Iris Cartwright was. Perhaps I should have read that chapter on the World Environmental Crisis instead of just taking the test. "If they try to get us to switch rooms again I'll invent some fictitious disease."

The smile on Rianne's face corroded. "No need to do that. Neither of those two snobs would be caught dead rooming with me." She indicated her legs. "They'd be afraid that my poverty might rub off."

"I think they're already afraid," I said thoughtfully. "I think each one is terrified that she'll be the one to lose and the other one will cast her out without a penny."

"Maybe," Rianne said. "But I still don't want to room with either of them."

"Me either. Besides," I said cynically, "they'll sleep better if they can keep an eye on each other. Otherwise the other one would always be wondering if her clone was up to something."

I sent an e-mail to Anaximander requesting some more stylish clothes and colored contact lenses—nothing too outrageous, blue and brown—then did a net search on Timothy's kidnapping. To my consternation, nothing came up no matter what search terms I used.

A commotion in the hall made me jump guiltily. "Timothy Castellan must be home." I shut off my palmtop. "Want to come see?" I asked Rianne.

"Sure. I wouldn't want to miss SilverDiaper," she said sarcastically.

"SilverDiaper?"

"That's what the tabloids call him because he's a rich kid." Rianne wheeled her way into the hall.

I followed her but put my hand on the back of her chair to stop her, when I realized Graciana and Timothy were arguing.

"Mr. Timothy, aren't you going to listen to the message?"

"Why? It's obvious what she's going to say. She promised she'd be home," Timothy Castellan said dully.

I recognized him from the data file Anaximander had given me. He had dark blond hair, watery gray eyes, and would have been taller than me if his shoulders hadn't been rounded with despair. His clothes were fashionable enough—a short-sleeved red shirt with a zebra tie and black linen pants—but they were rumpled and he looked uncomfortable in them, giving him a geeky look. Definitely not the snooty rich boy I'd feared.

Graciana looked compassionate and patient. "And she will be here. She wouldn't miss your symposium. She's just going to be later than she expected."

"She's *always* late," Timothy muttered.

Just then Graciana saw us. "Mr. Timothy, your guests are here."

Left with no other choice, I put on a smile and came forward to introduce myself.

"I'm Timothy Castellan." He shook my hand absently but didn't appear to see me. He gawked openly at Rianne's wheelchair. Rianne became angry again, snatching her hand back after Timothy shook it.

I rushed into the silence. "So are you planning to go to Dr. Keillor's talk on Martian geology tomorrow?"

"I wouldn't miss it. He's been studying Mons Olympus, Mars's biggest volcano, you know."

"We'll have to sit together, then." I smiled.

The invitation seemed to surprise Timothy. "That would be one hundred percent great!"

"By the way, just to warn you, our other roommates are a bit—" I paused, searching for the right word.

"—weird," Rianne said for me.

"—focused," I substituted.

"Obsessive," Rianne corrected.

"Have you heard of Iris Cartwright?" I asked.

Timothy nodded. I must be the only person in the world not to know who she was.

"Well, they're her clones, and their inheritance depends on their grades, so they're a bit competitive."

"Self-centered is more like it." Rianne rolled her eyes, relaxing out of her earlier stiffness.

Timothy blew it. "So what's wrong with your legs, anyhow? How come you don't have Augments?"

Rianne's face froze. "Not everyone was born stinking rich." She wheeled her chair around and left.

Timothy blinked, gray eyes bewildered. "I was just asking."

"She's a little touchy about her legs. Don't worry, she'll be okay in the morning." I hoped.

"Do you know what's wrong with her legs? I didn't think anybody had to use wheelchairs anymore, no matter how poor. Her parents' employers should have covered the cost." Timothy looked genuinely troubled, and it occurred to me that he was somewhat naive.

"She hasn't told me, and I'm not going to ask," I said firmly.

"It's not right." Timothy frowned stubbornly. "I'll ask my mother to arrange an operation for her."

His generosity to a girl he'd just met staggered me. I couldn't help liking him, even if he had the tact of a charging rhino.

"That's a very nice idea, but you might want to wait until she knows you a bit better before you do that," I said gently.

"Why?"

"Because she might refuse."

The possibility boggled him. "Why would she do that?"

"Pride," I said. From what I had seen Rianne had a lot of pride.

Timothy looked puzzled.

If he didn't get it, I couldn't explain it to him. I asked him a question about Mars, and he took the bait happily, talking for long minutes about making Mars habitable for humans outside of domes. "People think terraforming Mars means turning it into Earth's double, but that simply isn't possible. All you have to do is look at Mars's pink sky to know that."

"Have you actually been to Mars, then?" I asked. If anyone could afford to go for a pleasure trip it was the son of SilverDollar's president.

It was a simple question, but Timothy's expression changed. Shuttered. "Maybe," he said, and started talking about carbon dioxide levels.

I struggled not to show my astonishment. How could you not know for sure if you'd been to Mars? The journey took over a month and would be momentous. I imagined that one's first sight of an alien planet would be branded into memory forever.

Unless he'd been blindfolded. When Timothy was kidnapped had he been held somewhere in space, possibly on Mars?

CHAPTER

8

HE'S NOT DEAD, was all I could think as I stared at Michael Vallant the next morning. He was the last person I had expected to see when I stepped into the hallway.

I barely heard Graciana's introduction: "Miss Angel, this is Mr. Michael, the fifth finalist. You show him around? I make breakfast."

My knees felt weak as I anxiously studied Mike. He didn't look insane, either. In fact, he looked much better than the last time I'd seen him, no longer sleepless and haggard. His dark hair looked thick and vital, and he had shaved. His movements held only a faint remaining stiffness from his ordeal in the Loyalty Induction chamber.

There was a small bandage on his temple, just where my own had been. The Loyalty chip had clearly been installed, but was it working or was he free?

"Michelangelo," he said, his violet eyes dancing.

"Michael plus Angel. You did it. The chip doesn't work."

I bit my lip to keep from crying in relief. Mike held out his hands, and I gripped them both hard.

I experienced a small flash of memory—*running up and hugging him only to find his embrace unenthusiastic and brief*—and then the drowning memory overtook me again.

I opened my mouth in a soundless gasp, surfacing, and found Mike watching me with a frown on his face. I pulled away.

"What is it?" Mike asked.

I considered playing dumb, but something told me Mike wouldn't be put off. "I remembered something. I hugged you, but you didn't hug back. You weren't happy to see me."

Mike swore. "Of all things you would have to remember that."

I waited.

"Remember when I told you that I failed you once? The two of us were separated, and Dr. Frankenstein convinced me—briefly—that you had betrayed me. As soon as I saw you, I knew he had lied. You hugged me, and I realized I'd betrayed you, not the other way around."

I looked at Mike. He looked sincere. Sorry. But I didn't know if I could believe him. *Violet eyes lie.*

I dodged into shallower waters. "So you're the fifth finalist. Did Anaximander make you write an essay, too?"

Mike didn't let me get away with the retreat. He took my hand.

I resisted the urge to yank my hand away, keeping my voice cool. "Yes?"

"You and I may need to confer regularly." Mike bent his head, his voice a low whisper in my ear that sent a frisson of awareness racing up my spine. "I think we should pretend to be attracted to each other so we have an excuse for spending time together . . . alone."

His suggestion made sense, so I nodded. But inside my nerves were shrieking. I didn't want to. I didn't trust him. And I was all too aware that an attraction wouldn't be pretense.

"By the way, this is for you." Mike held out a flat package. "Anaximander said something about clothes?"

I snatched it from him. "Thanks. I'll be right back." In my room, I exchanged my plain dark green shirt for a pretty royal blue one with a scoop neck and plunked in blue contacts.

Dahlia and Zinnia came downstairs just as I came back out, and I introduced Mike to them, correctly deducing which clone was which from Zinnia's white hair and more conservative clothes. Today Dahlia's hair was black with red tips to match her wraparound red zebra-striped dress. I flinched when I saw her eyes. Color coordination might be fashionable, but, in my opinion, red contacts made her look freaky and inhuman. Bestial. Zinnia's white eyes weren't much better.

"I'm hungry," Dahlia said to Mike. "Have you eaten yet?"

"Yes."

Dahlia pouted. "Well, come have breakfast with us anyway. Graciana said she would make fresh orange juice." She meant the words to be cajoling,

but the red glint in her eyes made them seem
ominous instead.

Mike accepted anyway. "Sure." He turned from
Dahlia to smile at me. "Let's all go in to breakfast."

Within fifteen minutes Rianne and Timothy had
also joined us at the dining room table.

Dahlia kept trying to flirt with Mike; he
responded politely but saved his best smiles for
me. And his best smiles were heart-meltingly good.
On his lips, my name became an endearment.

I tried to tell myself that it wasn't real, that he
was only pretending to like me, but I didn't believe
it. Worse, I didn't want to believe it.

Rianne turned out not to be a morning person.
When Timothy moved one of the chairs so she
could park her wheelchair, she snapped at him. "I
can do it myself!"

Timothy blinked, looking bewildered. "I was
just trying to help."

"Well, don't."

Coming from such a tiny person, I found
Rianne's surliness amusing, a princess snarling at
her subjects.

Mike distracted Timothy by asking him about
the symposium. Ten minutes later, Timothy was
still talking happily, his banana muffin forgotten
on his plate.

I exchanged a laughing look with Mike before
leaving the two of them to bond. Rianne went with
me back to our room.

"He likes you," Rianne announced. "Too bad for
Dahlia."

I smiled and flopped on the bed. "You think so?
He's pretty cute, isn't he?"

Rianne nodded enthusiastically. "One hundred percent."

I bounced back into a sitting position, grinning besottedly. "You made a conquest, too. Timothy likes you."

I'd meant to be teasing, but Rianne surprised me by getting upset. "He does not!"

I remembered the way Timothy looked at Rianne and how he'd gone on and on about Mars, trying to impress her. "Actually," I said seriously, "I think he does. Why, don't you like him?"

"He's a rich snob!" Rianne burst out.

My eyebrows went up in surprise. "Really? I think he's kind of sweet. Geeky, but sweet."

"He's condescending."

I shrugged. "Hey, if you don't like him, you don't like him. We're only going to be here four days."

I enjoyed Dr. Keillor's talk on Martian geology, but I wished he had spent more time talking about its monstrous volcanoes and canyons and less time talking about its ice caps.

Standing in line for lunch afterward, I spied Anaximander crossing the food court. "Save a place for me," I told Rianne. "I left something in the auditorium." I took off after Anaximander. I had a bone to pick with him.

"Why wasn't I told that Timothy was kidnapped last year?" I asked when I caught up with him in the hall.

"It wasn't relevant," Anaximander said calmly. "You're here to learn about Mars, that's all."

"That's not true. Eddy placed me and Mike in the

Castellan household deliberately," I said. "Why?"

"I can't answer for Mr. Castellan."

I ground out a word of frustration. "All Eddy said is that he's worried about Timothy and to 'keep an eye on him.'"

"Then that's all you need to know," Anaximander said.

"How can I judge Timothy's state of mind, if I don't know what happened to him? I need more information."

"I'll inquire about releasing the information to you."

In other words, no. "At least tell me who kidnapped him. Was it the Spacers?"

"Yes." Anaximander hesitated, then said softly, "They held him for six months."

My gut wrenched in sympathy. Six months was a long, long time to be held among strangers. "What was the holdup?" I asked, but Anaximander only shook his head.

"I really can't tell you any more."

"Just one more question. Is kidnapping a concern now?"

"Kidnapping is always a concern for the rich," Anaximander said unhelpfully.

I frowned. "If I were Timothy's mother, I'd be paranoid about it. Surround him with bodyguards."

"She'd like to," Anaximander said dryly. "Timothy refused. He wouldn't even accept electronic surveillance. All he has is a panic button."

Interesting. But I was running late. "Thanks. I'd better hurry back, before Rianne stops saving me a place in line."

"Who?" Anaximander said.

"Rianne. The black girl in the wheelchair," I said.

Anaximander's expression didn't change, but I had the oddest idea that it took him a moment to remember Rianne. Was something wrong with one of his Augments?

"Of course." Anaximander walked away.

I made a face at his back, then hurried back to the food court. Rianne had had to let a few people go ahead of her, so the two of us were the last ones to arrive at the table, but Mike immediately squeezed over to make room for me between him and Dahlia. She grudgingly moved her chair over a bare inch.

I smiled sweetly at her. "So have you guys decided what prize you'll choose if you win? The trip to Mars or the cash?"

"Mars." "Mars, of course." Zinnia and Dahlia spoke together.

Dahlia looked as though she'd swallowed a lemon when she realized that she and her sister had actually agreed.

"We—" Zinnia stopped. Bit her lip. Started again. "*I* want to see if the microbes that are being used to reverse the Blight can be adapted to work on Martian soil."

"And you?" I looked at Rianne.

"I'll take the money." Rianne was just as positive. Mike nodded agreement. "The money."

Timothy looked at Rianne and Mike in dismay. "But the trip to Mars is a once-in-a-lifetime opportunity!"

Rianne wasn't impressed. "So is receiving seventy-five thousand dollars. At least for most of us."

"What about you?" Zinnia asked me.

"I haven't decided yet," I said. I didn't need to decide, since Mike and I weren't true finalists. The winner had to be chosen from among the Flower Twins and Rianne. "My head says the money, but my heart says Mars."

Timothy beamed at me. "Go for it."

"Maybe I will." I did want to see Mars. I hoped Eddy kept his word and sent me there on assignment.

The six of us toured part of the Exhibition Hall together, then split up to attend the afternoon sessions. Mike, Rianne, and I went to one called Microfossils: Mars's Past Life, while the Flower Twins and Timothy took in one on Martian soil.

Microfossils turned out to be less interesting than they'd sounded. I took out my palmtop as the lecturer brought out his thirtieth rock sample, and the three of us wrote messages back and forth.

Me: What should we do tonight for fun?

Rianne: I think Timothy has a VR set. We could play games.

Me: We can play VR any night. Let's do something different. Something fun.

Mike: Let's see if Timothy has the keys to the Exhibition Hall. It would be fun to see the planetarium without a crowd around.

Rianne: Even if Timothy has the keys he'll never break the rules and let us in.

Me: Leave that to me. I think Timothy needs to have more fun. It would be good for him.

The lights came back up, the lecture ending. I closed the palmtop. Mike caught my elbow as we stood up. "What are you planning?" he whispered.

"Don't you think I can do it?" I challenged.

He laughed. "That was never in question." His confidence in me made me feel good.

But as it turned out, we weren't given a chance to corrupt Timothy that evening. Timothy's mother was home.

"Mother!" Timothy exclaimed when he saw her, both pleasure and irritation in his voice. "What are you doing here?"

If President Castellan had hoped for a warmer welcome, she hid it well. "My meeting ended early, and I grabbed an aircar. I wanted to see how you were doing."

Timothy bristled at what, to me, sounded like a perfectly innocuous comment. *"I'm fine."* His words had too much emphasis.

"Why don't you introduce me to our guests?" President Castellan was a cool customer. She didn't betray that she knew who Mike and I were by a flicker an eyelash. She murmured something to the Flower Twins about having been privileged to meet their progenitor once, instantly winning them over. They were the only two who didn't look secretly dismayed when President Castellan insisted on taking the six of us out for dinner at a fancy restaurant after a detailed tour of the Exhibition Hall.

At supper Zinnia wrung President Castellan dry, questioning her about her long-ago meeting with Iris Cartwright. Dahlia, too, seemed hungry for the smallest detail about their progenitor. It occurred to me that the two of them were orphans for all intents and purposes.

"She left us a tape library of herself," Zinnia

said. "Teaching tapes with lessons, but they're not the same."

"Of course not," President Castellan agreed, and then, for the four hundredth time that evening, she tried to draw out her son. For the four hundredth time, she failed. Timothy interpreted every remark she made as a personal criticism, shrinking further and further inside himself like a turtle. After a while, Timothy wouldn't even look at her, gazing into his barley soup instead.

Timothy and Rianne together made for a conversational black hole. From Rianne's awed looks at the china and crystal, I gathered that she felt intimidated. And typically, she didn't like the feeling and turned surly, rejecting Timothy's suggestions on what to order.

Thank God Mike was there to help me keep the conversation limping along.

I wouldn't have thought the evening could get worse, but it did. When Rianne and I came back from a trip to the ladies' room, we saw Eddy standing at the table. We hung back a moment.

"I just popped in to see how you were doing," Eddy was saying to a delighted Timothy. "Everything looks great."

His compliment was generic, but Timothy glowed under it. "Thanks!"

Timothy's mother looked grim. When she'd tried to compliment Timothy, he'd started to mumble about how it wasn't his fault the Martian waterways exhibit had flooded the floor below.

"I thought you were tied up with the Ramsey merger," President Castellan said, steel in her voice.

"I was, I am," Eddy said glibly. "I just flew down for the night; I'll be back in New York in time for breakfast. I couldn't miss my favorite nephew's symposium, after all!"

"But if you fly back tonight, you won't get to see any of it," Timothy protested.

"I wish I could see it, Timmy, but I've got to nail the Ramsey deal for your mother." Eddy neatly slipped the blame onto President Castellan.

Timothy looked pleadingly at his mother. "Couldn't somebody else handle it?"

President Castellan cast a scathing glance at Eddy, then turned to her son. "No, dear, I'm afraid not."

Timothy closed up again.

Eddy smirked at his half sister, unconcerned by the murder in her eyes. "Well, I've got to run now. Bye." Turning from the table, he saw me. He winked.

The idiot! I felt my face freeze. He was going to blow my cover! Had anyone else seen?

Rianne had.

I bent closer to her ear. "*Please* tell me that man didn't wink at me," I said through clenched teeth.

Rianne's lips twitched. "Sorry. He's one hundred percent smitten. In fact he's coming this way."

"Arrgh!" Eddy was indeed coming closer, smiling greasily. "Don't leave me alone with him," I whispered furiously. I held tight to the back of Rianne's wheelchair, chaining her in place.

"Hello, ladies. I'm Eddy Castellan, Timothy's uncle."

I shook his outstretched hand. "I'm Angel Eastland, and this is Rianne Beaulieu."

"Pleased to meet you. Hey, Timothy, why didn't you tell me your new roommates were knock-outs?" Eddy called over his shoulder.

Eddy's compliment unnerved me. My heart was rabbiting in my chest, and my hands felt icy. With a shock, I realized I was afraid. Of Eddy.

I didn't understand why. Eddy was a creep, and he had the power to fire me, but that didn't explain my reaction.

Timothy didn't know how to answer his uncle's rhetorical question. His fair skin flushed with embarrassment. "I didn't think of it. That is—"

Eddy cut him off, still beaming at Rianne and me. "Timothy's been doing a great job running the symposium, don't you think? He's been run off his feet, so don't keep him up partying every night, okay?" Eddy winked again, and then left the rest of the table sitting in stiff silence.

Half an hour later, we returned to the Castellan house. President Castellan started to excuse herself when Timothy put an old science fiction movie— what else?—on the big screen in the living room.

"Wait," Zinnia said, entering the room breath-less, "there's something I wanted to show you." She stopped the movie and put in her own disk. "This one's my favorite," she said shyly.

A severe-looking blond with a snub nose appeared on the screen. She looked familiar, but I couldn't place her. I assumed my memory had another hole in it, and I braced myself for the drowning that usually followed, but it didn't come. As the blond woman held up a child's shape-sorting toy, I realized that Zinnia and Dahlia had the same snub nose.

This must be Iris Cartwright, their progenitor.

"Don't show them that!" Dahlia was on her feet, embarrassed, as Iris Cartwright demonstrated how to push the various blocks through the correct slots, naming the color and shape of each block as she did so. "This is one of the baby tapes."

Zinnia ignored her, speaking to President Castellan. "I like this one because she smiles. . . . There! Did you see it?"

"I saw it," President Castellan said gently.

Dahlia rolled her eyes at her clone-sister's dorkiness. "So she smiled, so what?"

Rianne scowled at Dahlia and said to Zinnia, "You're lucky to have the tape. I used to have one of my dad singing me happy birthday, but it broke."

"Are we going to watch the movie or not?" Dahlia demanded.

Timothy obligingly started the movie again. "Watch this shot. *Mariner* hadn't been to Mars yet, so they still thought the Martian canyons were 'canals.' "

The movie was so bad it was funny. We threw popcorn at the screen whenever they said something wrong about Mars, even developing a rating system. One kernel was thrown for obscure facts, up to a handful for dead obvious ones, like the color of the sky.

One movie turned into a marathon. Timothy made chocolate milk shakes, and we all pigged out. Zinnia went to bed after the first movie. Dahlia started to fidget halfway into the second and left soon after.

I watched the first three movies but faked a

yawn and excused myself when Timothy put on a fourth. I caught Rianne's eye and signaled that she should follow me.

Mike saw and stood up, too.

"Oh, are you all leaving?" Timothy sounded disappointed. "I could play a different movie." He started to rifle through his disks. Timothy appeared to own all the Martian movies ever produced and to have seen every one of them.

I sent Mike a pleading glance.

"Sure," Mike said easily. "What movies have you got?"

Timothy was happily listing off titles when Rianne and I slipped out.

"What is it?" Rianne asked curiously.

"I need help with something. Remember earlier when I said I thought Timothy needed to have more fun? I want to play a prank on him. Something fun, not mean."

Rianne looked interested. "What did you have in mind?"

I told her, and she laughed.

Half an hour later, we finished. Every item in Timothy's room had been moved and smushed up against the left wall. Bed, desk, lamps, pictures, hanging model of Mars, everything. It looked as if a black hole had tried to suck up the room and failed. I brushed my hands together, pleased with myself.

My search of Timothy's room hadn't turned up any sign of suicidal tendencies. No guns, no razors, no death literature. Except for his Mars obsession and a too neatly made-up bed, which could probably be attributed to Graciana, his room could have passed for any teenage boy's.

"What about the closet?" Rianne asked.

"Good thought." I crossed the room and slid back the door—and my stomach dropped to my knees.

Timothy's mother had a right to be worried, after all. The reason the bed was so neat was because Timothy wasn't sleeping in it. A pillow and a blanket lay on the floor of his closet.

CHAPTER

I CLOSED THE CLOSET IMMEDIATELY, shielding it from Rianne's view. "On second thought, let's do Mike's room instead."

"Ooh, let's." Rianne grinned, in the spirit of things now.

If Timothy was sleeping in his closet, his nerves must be pretty on edge. I wanted to make sure that when he entered his room, he knew it was a prank and not something more sinister.

So Rianne and I tied all Mike's clothes together and strung them down the hall, before retreating to our bedroom. We turned off the lights and got into our beds, but left the door open a crack so we would be sure to hear their reaction.

Mike didn't disappoint me. "What the hell?" he said twenty minutes later when the movie ended and they turned in for the night.

"Are those your clothes?" Timothy sounded confused.

"Yes," Mike said. "And no, *I* didn't tie them

together. And I think we can rule out your mother and Graciana, too." He came and stood right by our doorway. "Hmmm, I wonder who could have done it?" he said loudly. "Could it possibly have been Angel and Rianne?"

In the bed across from me, Rianne stuffed her fist in her mouth to keep from laughing.

I faked a snore, making her shoulders shake all the more.

"Stop grinning," Mike told Timothy as he stooped to pick up the clothes. "You haven't checked your room yet. They might have put all your clothes on the roof."

"Me?"

The open astonishment in Timothy's face made me doubly glad I'd decided to play a trick on Mike, too. Now Timothy would feel included in the fun instead of singled out and picked on.

"Yes, you." Mike gave Timothy a little shove. "Open your door and let's see."

They stepped out of my range of vision so I got up and put my eye to the crack. I saw Timothy approach his door warily.

"What if it's booby-trapped?" Timothy whispered.

"Then you get wet."

Timothy turned the doorknob and pushed open the door without stepping inside. When nothing happened, he reached inside and flipped on the light.

The two boys stared inside. "How did they do that?" Timothy sounded dazed.

Mike clapped Timothy on the shoulder. "Well, it looks like your clothes are fine." They laughed.

Mike came back out into the hall; I retreated back into bed. "You know this means war, don't you?" he said loudly, standing in front of Rianne's and my door.

"How do you know it was Rianne and Angel?" Timothy asked. "It could have been Zinnia and Dahlia."

"Trust me," Mike said. "I know Angel. This is one hundred percent her style."

My smile faded. Mike knew my style, but I hadn't had any idea that I was someone who liked to play tricks until tonight.

The boys had their revenge the next morning when a beaming Graciana served Rianne and me omelets while everyone else had pancakes. "Mr. Timothy tells me you had an argument over who most likes spicy food. Here is my specialty, omelets. They are very hot."

Faced with hurting her feelings, Rianne and I both dug in.

I liked spicy foods, but Graciana had put in enough peppers to set fire to the plate. "Bring on the Tabasco sauce," I said gamely, as my eyes streamed. My tongue went numb halfway through, but I ate the whole omelet.

Rianne only managed half of hers before conceding the field to me. "It's very good," she told Graciana weakly.

As soon as Graciana left, Rianne aimed a killing glare at Timothy. She didn't seem to blame Mike at all. A mistake. I was pretty sure it had been Mike's idea—as sure as Mike had been about last night's prank being my style.

"It's time to go," Timothy said. "Where's Zinnia? Is she always late?"

"She'll be down in a minute," Dahlia said sharply. "And she wouldn't be late if you had a decent number of bathrooms."

I used the time while we waited to check my palmtop for messages. I found a brief recording from Anaximander: "Angel, go to the second-floor offices at 10:30 A.M. if you want answers to your questions." I couldn't tell from his expression if Eddy had released the information or if Anaximander was going behind his back.

I waited until everyone had picked a session to attend, then chose the one no one else had selected. Mike looked as though he wanted to change his mind and go with me, but I shook my head, and he didn't.

The session on the Martian atmosphere turned out to be more interesting than it sounded. I was fascinated to learn that greenhouse gases that were pollutants on Earth were actually good for Mars, helping to warm up the atmosphere. I left promptly at 10:25 A.M.—no point in irking Anaximander if he was bending over backward to help me.

But Anaximander wasn't waiting for me upstairs. Eddy was.

If I'd seen him before he saw me, I would have quietly turned around and gone back downstairs. As it was, he smiled and waved. I came closer, reluctantly.

There was nothing to be afraid of, but I was afraid. Was Shadow Angel trying to warn me?

"Anaximander tells me you've been asking about Timothy's kidnapping," Eddy said easily.

I nodded, sparing a brief hope that my request hadn't gotten Anaximander in trouble.

"I'll be glad to tell you more, but first, can you give me your impression of Timothy?"

"He's nice," I said. "Smart. A little shy until you get him going. He knows a lot about Mars." I sorted through my other impressions. *He's defensive around his mother, and for reasons that I don't understand, he worships you.* "A little naive," I finished.

"Did he seem depressed at all?" Eddy fished.

"No," I said firmly. Whatever was wrong with him, I was certain Timothy wasn't suicidal. "Maybe a little moody," I added, remembering his behavior toward his mother.

Eddy pounced on that. "Mood swings, huh?" He shook his head. His expression was sad, but I didn't believe it. I didn't believe Eddy had feelings for anybody but himself. "Damn it. I was hoping he was getting better. Did he seem stable to you? Not . . . violent in any way?"

I laughed—I couldn't help it, the idea was so far-fetched. "Timothy? No."

Eddy didn't like being laughed at. He looked annoyed.

Fear cut me off midchuckle. What was it about Eddy that was putting me so on edge? He was shorter than I was and heavier. Dumber, too. Anger overwrote fear. If he tried anything I'd throw him on his butt so hard, he'd bounce—

Eddy said something, but I didn't hear it. I blinked and changed the subject. "So, about Timothy's kidnapping, what did the Spacers want? Why did negotiations drag on for so long?"

"The Spacers demanded a great long list of impossible things. It took time to whittle their demands down to something reasonable." Eddy waved that off as unimportant. "Ever since Timothy was kidnapped, he's been obsessed with Mars. This whole symposium is his idea; his mother indulged him by letting him put it on. I can't help thinking it's unhealthy."

Eddy paused expectantly, but I didn't chip in with an agreement. Timothy's interest in Mars wasn't unhealthy; sleeping in his closet was unhealthy.

"What happened to Timothy while he was kidnapped?" I asked.

"We don't know." Eddy shook his head and tried to look sad. "Timothy won't speak of his time as a captive. I think the kid needs help, but his mother stopped making him see a psychologist when he asked her to."

Another slur on President Castellan. Eddy really hated her.

"Who knows?" Eddy sighed. "Maybe the kid just wants attention from his mother. God knows, he doesn't get much otherwise. She's never home."

He was laying it on a little thick, in my opinion. President Castellan had taken the time to actually look in on Timothy's symposium, unlike Eddy.

Eddy looked at his watch. "Well, this has been fun, but I have to run. Keep up the good work, Angel." He smirked, then turned on his heel and left.

What good work? I hadn't done anything.

I tried to call Anaximander on my palmtop, but I got a busy signal, so I recorded a brief video message. "You should have told me I was meeting Eddy, not you."

I walked back downstairs and discovered that the morning session had already ended. The chat with Eddy had taken longer than I'd thought. My stomach felt a little queasy, but I headed for the food court to find everyone else.

I saw Timothy standing in line by himself and joined him. After a couple of minutes, I managed to work the conversation around to Eddy. "Why don't your mom and uncle get along?"

"Uncle Eddy is fifteen years younger than my mother. They've never been close—Mom hates Eddy's mom, Grandpa's second wife. Plus Eddy got into some scrapes with the law when he was a teenager, and Mom had to bail him out and pay damages."

"What kind of scrapes with the law?" I asked.

"Minor stuff," Timothy said vaguely. "You know, getting drunk and stealing the school flag, that sort of thing. Anyhow, she still treats him like a kid. She doesn't understand that he's changed. If she even speaks his name her voice gets all icy." Timothy shivered as if he feared being on the receiving end of that ice himself.

Lunches paid for, the two of us looked around for the rest of the group. Rianne and Zinnia were still in line, but Dahlia was cozying up to Mike at a table near the Exhibition Hall. Today she looked witchy in black.

"Come on," she coaxed Mike. "Tell me what your grade point average is. At least give me a hint."

She was flirting with Mike. Jealousy sizzled through me.

I interrupted Mike's modest evasion. "You wouldn't tell anybody? Not even Zinnia?" I deliberately goaded Dahlia. "I thought twins always shared secrets."

Ink black eyes that appeared to be all pupils narrowed. Dahlia's glare scorched me. *"Zinnia is not my twin."*

"Oh, yeah, that's right." I nodded amiably. "The two of you are competing, aren't you? So who's winning so far?"

"I'm beating her." Dahlia smiled viciously, her red lipstick a bloody slash. "My average is 93.6, and hers is 93.1."

"A stunning victory," I said.

Dahlia didn't appreciate my tone of voice. "And what's your grade point average?"

"Ninety-six," I said. I was showing off, but it sure felt good. It was even true—sort of. I couldn't remember my high school grades, but I had a ninety-six percent average in the computer modules SilverDollar had made me take.

Dahlia's bottom jaw unhinged. Apparently, she'd had me pegged as someone dumber than her.

I felt smug, until I turned my head and saw Mike. Something tightened inside me. The Renaissance children were supposed to be supersmart. Was Mike smarter than I was?

I received a reply back from Anaximander that afternoon.

"I'm sorry, Angel. I would have told you if I could have that Eddy was going to be there." Anaximander's jaw knotted, as if he had to fight to get the words out. "It was required of me." The message ended, leaving me puzzled. Had Eddy ordered him not to tell me? Why?

Timothy's mother wasn't home that evening, so Operation Planetarium was put into effect. When Graciana called everyone to supper I lagged behind and caught Timothy's arm. "Do you have the keys to the Exhibition Hall? Could you possibly sneak Mike, Rianne, and me in tonight?"

Timothy frowned. "Why?"

I lowered my voice to a whisper. "It's for Rianne. She's dying to see the Mars Planetarium. When we went yesterday, it was too crowded. She can't stand up, so all she saw was other people's heads. We wouldn't touch anything," I swore. "We just want to see."

Timothy eagerly agreed. My plan worked so well, I almost felt guilty. He definitely liked Rianne.

"Don't tell her the trip's just for her," I cautioned Timothy. "She'll get all prickly on us. I told her I was going to ask you so Mike and I could have a semiromantic date."

Timothy nodded, and we went in to supper.

At midnight the four of us met in the hallway, talking in whispers. I hesitated with my hand on the doorknob. "Should we invite the Flower Twins?"

"Zinnia's all right," Rianne said unexpectedly. "You could ask her. But not Dahlia, please." She faked a shudder.

"Invite neither or both, but not just one," Mike said.

"Why?" Rianne wanted to know.

"Whoever you invite will take it as an insult. They're too close. Rejecting one is like rejecting the other."

"But they don't even like each other," Rianne said.

"Doesn't matter, they're sisters. Didn't you notice the way Dahlia zinged Timothy when he commented on Zinnia's running late this morning? They're allowed to criticize each other, but heaven help any outsider who steps in."

I nodded. Mike was right. "We won't invite them then."

The night outside had zoomed straight past cool and right into chilly. We cut ruthlessly across lawns instead of sticking to the paved paths. One of the lawns fought back; it had recently been watered, and everyone's shoes got soaked.

Timothy had a flashlight, but otherwise the Exhibition Hall was dark and rather spooky with its high-ceiling echoes and odd-shaped shadows.

We made it to the planetarium without breaking anything and went inside the small dome. Timothy started up the show, and we stood in the middle of an exotic Martian sunset. The sunset swiftly dimmed, and the Martian night sky with its two moons came out. Then that scene shifted to the view from Phobos. Mars was rust red, so different from Earth, with no clouds to obscure its arid beauty. For the first time I began to feel the pull it exerted on Timothy.

He and Rianne were speechless before it, and Mike quietly took me away from them to a different part of the dome. They would assume we were seeking some time alone, rather than giving them time alone. Classical music rose and fell, surrounding us in our own little bubble.

The question of Mike's intelligence had been burning in the back of my mind all day, and I couldn't resist asking him, "So what *is* your grade point average?"

My casual tone didn't fool Mike. He was silent a moment. "No, Angel," he said finally. "I'm not going to play that game with you again. We aren't rivals, and I won't let you use competition as an excuse to keep me at arm's length."

I opened my mouth to deny I'd done any such thing, and then realized he was right.

"Now can we talk about something important?" Mike said impatiently.

My face burned. "Of course. I talked to Eddy today and tried to pin down some more details about Timothy's kidnapping, but I didn't have much luck. He said the Spacers made 'unreasonable demands.' "

"When did you talk to Eddy?" Mike asked sharply.

"This morning." I explained about Anaximander's message to me. "I hope he's not in hot water over this."

Mike shook his head impatiently. "Don't waste your sympathy on him. Both he and Eddy are hiding something from us. But that's not what I meant by 'important.' " He put his hands on my shoulders. "Let's talk about us."

Only he didn't talk; he kissed me instead.

He took me by surprise, and I reacted instinctively, closing my eyes and kissing him back before jerking myself away. I was trembling, deeply dismayed by the way my body wanted to melt against his like plastic.

"Now tell me that you don't remember me," Mike said, satisfaction in his tone.

"I don't."

"Yes, you do."

He touched my cheek, and I caught his wrist, making him listen. "No, I don't," I said forcefully. "I'm sorry, Mike, but it's true. Shadow Angel may know you, *but I don't*. You can't expect me to have the same feelings for you that you do for me when I've only known you a few days."

Mike didn't heed my blunt warning, pouncing on the bit of information I'd let slip. "Shadow Angel?"

I ignored him and started talking about what Timothy had told me regarding President Castellan's relationship to her half-brother.

After a brief pause, Mike gave in, and we talked about Eddy.

The planetarium's show started to repeat itself after half an hour, and Timothy turned it off. I studied Rianne's face by flashlight glow to see if anything romantic had happened between her and Timothy. I didn't think it had, but there seemed to be a new harmony between them that pleased me.

The group's mellow mood lasted until Mike went to open the door and couldn't. "We're locked in," he said.

CHAPTER

10

OF COURSE, WE ALL PUSHED against the door to see
for ourselves, but Mike was right. The door had
been barred from the outside.

Mike sidled up to me while Timothy and Rianne
argued over who had entered last. "Is this part of
your matchmaking scheme by any chance?"

I shook my head. It hadn't occurred to me.

"Damn," Mike said.

I agreed one hundred percent. Being locked in
was no big deal. Worst case scenario, we were
found there in the morning and lectured by
Anaximander. No, what worried me was, who had
locked us in and why? Had someone followed us
to the Exhibition Hall? Dahlia, maybe, angry at
being left out? I preferred that thought to the grim
one that my midnight excursion might have
placed Timothy in danger. Was some would-be
kidnapper waiting outside for reinforcements?

"Okay," I said. "We're four smart people. Let's
figure a way out of here."

Rianne was all for cutting a way through the dome wall, but Timothy objected to damaging someone else's property. Timothy wanted to phone for help on his palmtop, but everyone else voted to leave that as a last resort.

In the end we followed Mike's plan. "Let's look around for another exit. There may be access to a catwalk or something."

We didn't find any staircases going up, but we did find a ladder going down. A trapdoor in the raised platform that housed the holoprojector led to it. Timothy shone the flashlight inside, but it was hard to tell if the crawl space went anywhere.

"I'll check it out." I swung my leg over the hole and climbed down. "I'm at the bottom," I called up a moment later. "Hand me the flashlight."

Timothy lay on his stomach and held out the flashlight, but I couldn't quite reach it. I jumped up and grazed it with my fingertips. Timothy thought I had it and let go.

Crash! One broken flashlight. Four blind people.

"Angel?" Mike called anxiously.

"I'm fine. I guess I'll have to explore by touch," I said.

"Move out of the way," Mike said. "I'm coming down."

I didn't think it was a good idea to leave Timothy undefended, but I couldn't say so. "There's not enough room," I said, but Mike didn't listen. I pressed my body against a wall to prevent myself from getting a foot in the face.

Once he was down, we stood back to back and felt the walls with our hands. I'd just gotten to the bottom of my wall when Mike said, "I found a tunnel, I think. It's pretty small."

I called up the news to Timothy. "We're going to go down a tunnel. Could one of you start counting so we can get a fix on your voices?"

Timothy began, a slight quaver in his voice. "One, two . . ."

Rianne joined in. "Three, four . . ."

I went first because I was smaller than Mike. I squirmed around, brushing Mike in the close quarters, then started down the tunnel on my stomach. I scraped my elbows on the rough cement. As a bonus, the tunnel was cold and dirty.

After only a few feet, I could no longer hear Timothy and Rianne counting.

"Watch for side passages," Mike said from down by my ankles.

But all I touched was machinery, the generator that made the holoprojectors go. At the end of the tunnel was a larger space; I sat up gratefully and kept feeling the walls. Nothing, nothing. The ceiling. "Bingo. There's another trapdoor."

I was afraid it would just bring us up back inside the planetarium, but we got lucky. When I cautiously put my head through I saw the faint illumination of the Exhibition Hall's sunroof. After that it was an easy matter to climb down from the platform and go around to open the door by removing the length of heavy pipe that had been shoved through the double door handles. Mike stayed outside just in case the mischief-maker was still around.

I followed the sound of voices.

"Eight hundred and fifty-six," Timothy was saying.

Rianne had stopped counting. "They haven't replied. I think we should go look for them."

"No need," I said cheerfully. "We made it out. Come on."

They didn't have to be asked twice. Twenty minutes later we were safely back in the Castellan house, without having seen any sign of the mysterious person who had locked us in.

Rianne covered her mouth to choke back giggles when we stepped into the porch light. I studied Mike's dirt-streaked appearance with resignation. "I suppose I look just as bad as him?"

"Worse," Rianne said. "You're blond. At least you used to be."

Timothy and Rianne had gone to bed by the time Mike and I took turns using the bathroom. "Good night." I sent Mike a friendly smile.

But he wanted more. His soft voice caught me in the hall. "I want her back. The other Angel. I won't stop until I find her." And, devastatingly, "I miss her."

Something of what I was feeling must have shown on my face, because when I came in Rianne sat up in bed. "Angel? Is something wrong?"

I sat down on the edge of my bed and started changing clothes. "Mike kissed me."

Rianne grinned. "Oh, yeah? Tell me more."

I shrugged. "He's a good kisser." I pulled on my nightgown.

A pause. "I thought you liked Mike."

Whoops. Now I was endangering our cover story. "I do," I said hastily. "It's just the usual relationship stuff. You know, does he like me as much as I like him? I mean, after this weekend I have no idea if I'll ever see him again."

"That's tough."

I turned off the light and climbed under the covers, but rolled over on my side so I could talk to Rianne across the space between our beds. "What do you think?"

"I've never had a boyfriend, so I'm the wrong person to be asking for advice," Rianne said.

"Never?" I couldn't believe it. Rianne might not be able to walk, but she was gorgeous. Fairy princess beautiful with wonderful high cheekbones.

Rianne gave a short, bitter laugh. "Yeah, strangely enough boys aren't attracted to the wheelchair."

I thought perhaps that her coming up short in the boyfriend department might have a bit more to do with the chip on her shoulder, but didn't say so.

"But if I were you," Rianne said, "I'd go for it. Speaking as someone who might drop dead at any time, I'd say don't waste your chances."

I was silent a beat. "Would you care to repeat that? What do you mean you could drop dead at any time?"

From the long pause before Rianne spoke again, I gathered that she hadn't meant to let that slip. "In addition to bad legs I also have a bad heart." Her voice was ultracasual. "When I was five, the doctors said I wouldn't live past sixteen. My mother had a similar condition, and she lived until she was thirty-five, but sooner or later a bad shock will do me in."

I was angry that she hadn't told me before—but I also knew that in her shoes I wouldn't have told anyone either. I sensed her holding her breath, waiting to see if the knowledge would change the way that I treated her, so I kept my words practical. "What do I do if you have an attack? Do you have medicine?"

"Yes. There's a vial of pills that I wear around my neck at all times. Give me two of them."

"Thanks for telling me," I said. "I think I'll take your advice. About Mike. I mean, if I don't give us a chance then I'll never know. Let me know if you change your mind about Timothy," I teased her. "You can fake a heart attack and make him give you the kiss of life!"

A pillow flew out of the dark and hit me on the head.

The next morning I watched Dahlia carefully, but she showed no awareness that the four of us had sneaked out. That left possibility number two, an enemy of Timothy's. Which meant I would have to tell Anaximander what had happened. The thought put me in a bad mood, and Mike made things worse.

"Well, I will say the food's decent working for SilverDollar," Mike said for my ears only after another huge breakfast courtesy of Graciana. "Remember back in March when we came home to find Anaximander in our apartment and had to skip town before payday? I was getting pretty tired of roast potatoes before you earned some cash baby-sitting."

A little Chinese girl giggling as I tickled her—

—and then I was falling through murky green water, drowning. Again.

Mike reached out to steady me, but I slapped his hands away. "Stop it," I said tightly. "You know I don't want to remember."

"Yes," Mike admitted. "But I don't know why you don't want to remember."

Instead of answering Mike, I went back into my bedroom and recorded a short message to Anaximander, confessing our midnight jaunt and telling him that someone had shut us in. On the walk to the symposium, I was as cool to Mike as I could be without making Rianne and Timothy wonder if we'd had a fight.

Mike didn't take the hint, lacing his fingers through mine. "Boy, you must be mad at me. You took off your angel pendant."

My hand flew to my neck, but it was bare. "Where is it? What happened to it?" I forgot my annoyance at Mike, dismayed.

Mike studied me warily. "I assumed you took it off before we left the house."

"Was I wearing it at breakfast?" I got down on my hands and knees and brushed my fingers across the pavement.

"I don't know if you were wearing it at breakfast." Mike crouched down beside me. "So you really lost it? You weren't trying to draw my attention to your bare neck?"

I frowned. "What do you mean?"

Mike frowned back at me. "You were touching your neck. Fiddling with your collar. I thought you wanted me to notice you'd taken off the pendant."

"No." My hand crept up there now. My neck felt naked. I had worn the angel pendant Mike had given me for Christmas night and day since coming to work for SilverDollar, never taking it off.

And what did that say about my feelings for Mike?

I avoided pursuing that thought. "Think back. When did you last see it?"

"I don't know. Maybe yesterday at breakfast, or supper the night before. Don't worry about it. The chain probably broke and it fell on the floor. Graciana will find it when the robots clean your room."

I wasn't reassured. What if I'd lost it somewhere else?

Rianne, Timothy, and Zinnia had stopped ahead of us. "What's wrong?" Rianne called.

"I lost my angel pendant," I called back. "Have any of you seen it?"

They all came back to help me search, even Dahlia, but none of them could remember for sure when they had last seen it. Timothy had never noticed it at all.

"Angel, please don't worry about it." Mike pressed my hand. "I'll buy you another one."

I shook my head, fighting back panic. He didn't understand. The angel pendant was special to me, yes, but the main reason I was upset was because I was afraid the missing pendant meant another memory loss. It was bad enough that I had almost no memory of my life before my Loyalty Induction; it was intolerable to think that the memory loss was still continuing, that I would continue to forget more and more.

* * *

At lunch, I stood in line with Timothy, more to avoid Mike than out of any real desire for a chili dog. I looked around restlessly—

—and my gaze collided with that of a man who stood one line over and five people farther back.

Several small things about him grated on my instinct.

He was the wrong age: ten years older than the students, but younger than most presenters. His hair was black, the curling ends long enough to brush his collar; his coloring and features were a mix of Spanish and Indian. He was very handsome. And he had silver eyes.

I remembered what Anaximander had told me, about almost all Spacers having Augments of some kind.

The man looked directly at me. Even though I'd caught him staring, he didn't look away or smile or look embarrassed.

I broke eye contact as casually as I could and tapped Timothy on the shoulder. "Do you see that man back there? The one with the silver eyes? Do you know him?"

Timothy looked. "No. Should I?"

"I guess not." I shrugged off my disappointment. So much for my brief fantasy of bringing down one of the Spacers that had kidnapped Timothy. Not everyone with silver eyes was a Spacer—as Anaximander himself illustrated.

We got our chili dogs, but as we were leaving, the man intercepted us. "Are you Timothy Castellan? My name is Seth Lopez. I just wanted to tell you what a wonderful job I think you've done here."

Timothy shook his hand, pleased. "You really think so? Thanks!"

Seth loaded on the compliments for several more minutes, making Timothy blush, but I didn't buy it. I watched uneasily as Seth leaned forward. He was too intense, full of repressed triumph. "Can I ask you something, Timothy?"

"Sure," Timothy said easily. "What?"

"How did you feel when—"

My hand moved before my brain had time to analyze why, drawing back my iced tea—

"—when the Spacers abducted you?"

—and dashing it across Seth's face and eyes.

CHAPTER

11

TIMOTHY BLINKED REPEATEDLY, stunned by Seth's unexpected question and my actions. Silence rippled through the crowd around us, as everyone turned to see what was going on.

Seth wiped a hand across his dripping silver eyes but kept staring at Timothy instead of me, the girl who'd thrown iced tea in his face. My hunch became a sure thing. Seth was a tabloid reporter, and his silver eyes hid a video camera, an illegal cosmetic Augment, a boon to his job, not a medical necessity. "Is it true—" Seth started.

My mind worked like lightning. "Food fight!" I yelled, drowning out the rest of Seth's question.

"—that your mother refused to pay your ransom?"

I threw Timothy's green slurpie in Seth's eyes, but that was only a temporary solution, so I dumped my chili dog over Timothy's head. Red meat sauce turned his blond hair orange and streaked his face. He looked almost unrecognizable. Good.

Working swiftly, I showered my French fries on the couple at a nearby table and spilled a standing boy's drink over his shirt and pants. That seemed to do the trick.

"Food fight!" Five different voices chorused, and the air was suddenly full of flying hamburgers.

Timothy was still standing there like a lump. I grabbed his hand and yanked him into a run. I deliberately bumped into people as we went, spreading confusion.

Not about to let his big story get away, Seth gave chase, still yelling questions—"Why were you held so long? Is it true you've been seeing a shrink?"—but nobody paid any attention to him in the chaos.

I snatched someone's waffle cone and threw gobs of ice cream like snowballs over my shoulder on the run. Chocolate smeared Seth's shirt and hair. A girl shrieked as a miss splattered on her bare arms.

A bucket of fried chicken provided me with two minutes' worth of firepower. I thwacked Seth's forehead and chest with wings and drumsticks. He got really mad and ran faster, but slipped on someone else's taco spill.

Timothy was gasping, whether from shock or our breathless run, I couldn't tell. I felt great myself and laughed as a random hot dog hit my shoulder.

A knot of people squirting each other with squeeze bottles of mustard and ketchup blocked our way. I pulled Timothy up onto a table, but for the first time Seth got close enough to grab my leg. I rubbed a mayo-covered bun on his face, kicked him, and scrambled on.

Then we were out of the food court. I pulled Timothy inside an empty lecture hall and locked it.

One look at Timothy's gray, stricken face killed my excitement. "Here, sit down." Alarmed, I urged him into a red, plush seat. He collapsed into it and put his face in his hands.

I studied him anxiously. He didn't seem to be crying, so I decided to give him a moment to recover. I pulled out my palmtop and called Anaximander. Hopefully, Timothy would be too shocked to realize that I knew whom to call.

Anaximander's face appeared. "Angel, please call back. There's a—"

"—food fight going on," I finished. "I know. I started it. Some guy calling himself Seth Lopez was asking Timothy rude questions about his kidnapping. I think he was a tabloid reporter. Can you catch him?"

For an answer, Anaximander hung up. I decided that meant he was going to try so I went and sat by Timothy.

"No one's supposed to know," Timothy said, the first words he'd spoken since Seth asked him about being kidnapped. Seth might as well have hit him with a tire iron; his words had had the same effect.

"Know what?" I asked gently.

"About the kidnapping." Timothy stared off blankly. "It was hushed up. Now my face will be all over the tabloids." Timothy sounded doomed. "Everyone will see me."

I could at least help him with that worry. "No, they won't. All they'll see is you smiling. Seth won't have any video of your reaction because I threw my drink in his eyes. His tape will be blurred and splattered. And the later shots of you will be unrecognizable because of the chili dog I dumped in your hair."

"Oh. Is that why you did that?" Timothy looked briefly cheered, before sinking back into depression. "But the story will still come out. And then everyone will *look* at me. They'll stare and stare . . . *I can't bear it.*"

"Your mom will protect you." I offered all the crumbs I could think of. "It will blow over."

Timothy wasn't listening, trapped in a nightmare. "There will be cameras everywhere, watching me, recording me in secret." He shuddered.

"It will blow over," I repeated. I looked toward the door. Had Anaximander caught Seth? Maybe they could work some deal with him, pay him off for not selling the story to the tabloids.

"The only way I could stand it the first time was because almost no one knew. Now everyone will. Even the people who are too polite to mention it will know. It will be there in their eyes when they look at me."

"What will be in their eyes?" I asked.

"The curiosity. The wondering. What happened to him all those months? Did he crack?" Timothy spoke about himself in the third person, making the hairs stand up on the back of my neck. "Is he crazy?"

"No one who knows you will think that." Unfortunately, I couldn't vouch for strangers.

"My mother looks at me funny," Timothy muttered.

A minefield loomed in front of me. "Your mom is worried about you. That doesn't mean she thinks you're crazy." I tried a smile. "My mom worries about me all the time. That's what moms do."

A twinge passed through me. Was my mom worried about me? I didn't know.

"Not *my* mother," Timothy said bitterly. "If Uncle Eddy hadn't rescued me, she'd still be haggling over my ransom."

I was still struggling with that revelation when a knock came at the door. "It's Anaximander."

I opened the door and let Mike and Anaximander in. Mike was with him. "Did you catch him?" I asked.

"He escaped." Anaximander turned to Timothy. "I apologize for the security breach. It won't happen again."

Timothy's face reddened with anger. "How do you know that? If he got past you once, he can get past you again!" He shoved Anaximander, and I suddenly remembered Eddy's hints that Timothy might be violent.

No, I didn't believe that. Timothy had a right to be upset. Being angry didn't make him violent.

Anaximander questioned Timothy and me about what had happened, then escorted Timothy to a washroom so he could clean up. I had escaped with only minor mustard stains, and Mike wasn't too messy either, so we stayed behind.

My brows drew together in a frown when I realized that Anaximander hadn't congratulated me on my quick thinking in preventing Seth from getting Timothy on video. Of course, he hadn't lectured me over the planetarium incident either. I should probably count myself ahead, but it still rankled.

"You know," I said to Mike, "sometimes I get the feeling that Anaximander doesn't want me to succeed."

"Of course he doesn't," Mike said, startling me. "He knows you're his replacement."

"What?"

"Out with the old, in with the new. Before the violet-eyed, the Augmented were top of the line when it came to espionage. Not anymore," Mike said.

"Mr. Castellan likes to have the newest toys," Anaximander had said. I had thought he'd been referring to the Black Panther aircar. Had there been a slight bite to his words, a double meaning? I couldn't remember.

"It must really gripe him," Mike continued, "knowing that once he's trained you, he'll be tossed out like an old piece of garbage."

"You don't know that," I said.

Mike shrugged. "No, but it makes sense. As you said, SilverDollar is a company, not a government. How many espionage agents—sorry, I mean *security investigators*—does it need?"

I studied his face, trying to decide whether I could believe him or not.

"You don't trust me, do you?" Mike asked softly.

"I don't know you well enough to trust you," I said sadly.

A tiny flinch and then his face smoothed out. "Then maybe it's time you got to know me," he said cryptically.

We told Rianne and the Flower Twins that there had been a problem with a reporter but didn't mention the kidnapping. Timothy rejoined us for the last half of the afternoon session on genetically adapting humans to Mars instead of terraforming Mars, but remained in a bad mood.

After the lecture, the presenter, Dr. Hatcher, came up to me. "Excuse me, are you Angel Eastland?"

"Yes," I said, startled. My heart gave an extra pound. Was I supposed to know who he was? Dr. Hatcher was in his forties. He had a lean build and graying brown hair. The few lines on his face gave him a grave, intelligent air. He didn't look familiar and sparked no drowning flashes.

Dr. Hatcher smiled at me. "I read your essay and was very impressed by it. I'd like to discuss a few of your ideas, if you have the time."

I barely remembered what I'd written, but it would have been rude to say no. "Of course." I waved Mike and the others on. "Are you one of the judges, then?"

"Not exactly." He didn't elaborate, going on to talk about several of the points I dimly remembered writing about.

I responded as best as I could. I was about to excuse myself when he suddenly changed tack.

"Tell me, Angel, do you know what you want to do with your life?"

Since my employment by SilverDollar was a secret from Timothy, I thought it best not to tell him I had an exciting career as a security investigator. "I haven't really made up my mind yet," I stalled.

"Any strong possibilities? Medicine? Theater? Business?"

His eyes were kind, I thought suddenly.

A stupid way to think. How could eyes be kind? But somehow his were.

I shook my head. I'd never given any of those careers the slightest thought.

"Let me rephrase the question," Dr. Hatcher said. "What do you enjoy doing? What kind of job would you find fun?"

I thought back over the last week. I'd enjoyed racing Anaximander through the maze—and winning. I'd enjoyed flying the Black Panther. I'd enjoyed playing a prank on Mike. I'd enjoyed outwitting Seth.

"I like being . . . challenged," I said at last.

Dr. Hatcher nodded as if he had expected my answer. "Here's my card. When you decide on a career, give me a call. I guarantee my employer would be interested in sponsoring your education."

"Thanks." I pocketed his card.

"You're a very special person, Angel. Never sell yourself short," Dr. Hatcher said intensely.

I stared for a moment. What was going on here? I had the distinct and uneasy impression his words had a hidden meaning.

Dr. Hatcher was waiting for a reply.

"I won't," I mumbled.

A hint of disappointment showed on his face. He soldiered on. "If anyone treats you badly, please feel that you can come to me for help."

Fat chance, I thought. "Of course." A small pause. "I should go catch up with my friends now."

"Of course," Dr. Hatcher said, but he looked sad.

What the hell had that been about? Kind eyes or not, there was something not quite right about Dr. Hatcher.

Mike was waiting for me outside, but everyone else had already returned to the Castellan house.

"So what did he want?" Mike asked. It was super windy outside so we took a motorized walkway.

"To offer me a job, apparently." I related our conversation. "But there was something else, some undercurrent." I frowned, trying to put my finger on what had raised my hackles and failing. "Well, I guess it doesn't really matter since I already have a career."

"You're happy working for SilverDollar then?" Mike asked.

His question made me uneasy. "Of course." I was, wasn't I?

"The old Angel was opposed to becoming what she was genetically engineered to be," Mike said.

Curiosity reared its ugly head. "What did I want to do?"

Mike hesitated. *He didn't know.* "You said once that you could always be a dancer."

A dancer. I considered it. I enjoyed dancing, and choreography sounded like fun. But. "Wouldn't that be a waste of my talents?"

My answer made Mike angry. "The Angel I knew would rather be a waitress than be forced to do something she didn't want to do."

The old Angel sounded as if she would cut off her nose to spite her face. "I don't think I'd care to wait tables my whole life," I said lightly.

Mike didn't smile. What I saw in his eyes was very close to despair.

CHAPTER

12

GRACIANA HADN'T FOUND my angel pendant. She promised to check the robots' dust bins, but I wasn't hopeful.

To distract myself during supper, I asked Zinnia what she planned to take at university.

Zinnia looked surprised that I'd even asked. "Microbiology, of course." Following in Iris Cartwright's footsteps again.

"That's nice," I lied. It still seemed creepy to me: being forced into a career by a dead woman—*and wasn't that what Mike had meant when he'd said that old Angel hadn't wanted to be a superspy because she'd been genetically designed to be one?*

"What do you mean?" Dahlia asked suspiciously. "Nice?"

I had to scramble to remember what I'd last said. "Oh, just that I'm glad you'll both have a job. I was afraid that only the winner would be allowed to join the family firm."

Silence at the table.

"There's no job provided for the loser in Iris Cartwright's will," Zinnia said finally.

I was beginning to seriously dislike Iris Cartwright, hero or not. "But whoever wins will have the power to hire whomever she wants, right?" I asked.

"Hire *and* fire!" Dahlia said with relish.

Zinnia paled. "You're only up by four tenths of a percentage point. Don't assume you'll be the boss."

Dahlia narrowed her eyes at her clone sister. "Maybe I'll let you sweep out the labs. I wouldn't want you to starve."

"I don't need your charity. I can name ten corporations that would love to hire me!"

"Great, then you're both set," Mike said heartily. "Dahlia, could you please pass the rice? I'm still hungry."

I almost asked Rianne what career she was planning, before I remembered: when Rianne grew up she would be dead. My throat choked up.

Just then Rianne and Timothy got into an argument over how many moons Jupiter had. In my opinion, Rianne didn't even care. She just wanted to argue. Specifically, she wanted to argue with Timothy.

By the end of the meal only Mike and I were still speaking to everyone.

The tense atmosphere should have made for a lousy evening, but instead I had a blast because of Mike. He poured forth energy like a supernova, and the rest of us caught fire in turn. "This is our last evening here. Let's make it a fun one, okay?"

Timothy wanted to play VR Alien Invasion. Rianne countered with VR Sword and Sorcery.

Zinnia diffidently suggested VR Molecule World, but when Mike proposed World-Building we all fell into line. Rianne didn't even fuss about being carried into the basement by Mike and Timothy.

We all donned VR goggles and strapped on VR bodysuits. Our virtual bodies appeared in the game environment, the images playing on our goggles translating into a fair approximation of reality. The images had a slightly flat, cartoonish quality to them, and the sense of touch was limited to pressure, but it was still amazing.

Each of us designed a world and then showed it off to the others. The evening became a string of wonderful moments:

—walking up a staircase that turned sideways and twisted like an Escher painting, disorienting us, so that we suddenly realized we were walking on the underside of the stairway we had climbed before.

—drifting through a zero-G swimming pool designed by Rianne with bubbles of water that floated free and could be pushed together to form larger bubbles, miniature worlds equipped with tropical fish. Kissing Mike and having a large bubble suddenly envelop us. Kissing in VR wasn't anything like the real thing, of course, but it was still fun.

—falling over laughing after plunging through a trapdoor into an exercise class run by the Spanish Inquisition. "You, there, on the rack! Give me ten push-ups!"

Mike flirted with me the whole game, and I used the excuse of being undercover to flirt back.

The surprise was Rianne's behavior. Her VR

body wasn't confined to a wheelchair, and she ran wild, laughing more than I'd ever seen her and pelting Timothy with green goo. He chased her and finally managed to tackle her and rub goo in her hair. Rianne retaliated by tickling him.

I watched them curiously: did Rianne like him after all? Timothy looked as though he was trying to decide if he should kiss her. I thought he would chicken out, but he didn't, putting his lips on hers.

Rianne froze. I hoped the VR kiss wasn't her first kiss.

Timothy drew back, looking unsure.

A moment later Rianne ended the game, saying she was tired. By the time Mike and I carried her and her wheelchair back upstairs, Dahlia, Zinnia, and Timothy had also called it a night. I found myself alone with Mike.

"Well," I said, with equal parts nervousness and reluctance, "I suppose we ought to say good night, too."

"Play one more game with me." Mike's violet gaze caught and held mine. "For our cover story."

"Okay," I said. "More World-Building?"

"Nah. Something faster." Mike's eyes glinted.

I was immediately suspicious. "Like what?"

"Badminton."

I poked at the idea from all sides but couldn't spot a trap, and I wasn't about to back down from the challenge in Mike's tone. "You're on." We donned the headsets and gloves again.

I had expected to play against Mike, but to my surprise he set up the game as a mixed doubles match against the computer. He selected Expert level, and a man and woman appeared on the virtual badminton court. They introduced themselves as Josie Farber and Paul Shinn. A discreet line of text identified them as last year's Olympic champions.

I fully expected to get creamed—I was athletic, but I couldn't remember ever playing badminton before—but as soon as Mike and I walked onto the court magic happened. Without consulting each other, we took up positions, me on the left, Mike on the right. Mike served first, a hard drive skimming over the net, and as soon as I heard the twang of his racket striking the birdie, I was moving up to the left corner of the net. When Josie slashed forward to return Mike's serve, I was there to spike it back over the net for our first point.

When it was my turn to serve, the same thing happened. Mike knew exactly where the return shot would go. The volley lasted longer this time, and on the third whizzing return sent to me by Paul, I wound up my arm as if to spike the birdie. Then I ducked, and Mike did a powerful backhand clear that left Josie scrambling and won us another point.

Instead of serving again, I held the birdie over my racket and looked at Mike, obscurely troubled.

He looked pleased. "Your reflexes trust me," he said softly. "Listen to them."

I stopped dead. "What's going on?"

"You and I used to play badminton. Coach Hrudey was training us for the Olympics."

His words had the impact of a club hitting my head. *An icy shock to my flesh as I fell into cold water. Sinking down, down, through murky green depths. Holding my breath and flailing my limbs,*

*until finally the pressure in my chest grew too great
and I involuntarily gasped in water. Choked—*

"Angel?"

I heard Mike's concerned voice, and then he
ripped off my headset, and I found myself back in
the basement, dry as unbuttered toast. I shuddered, remembering the heavy sensation of liquid
filling my lungs.

"Angel, what is it? What happened?" Mike
slipped an arm around my shoulders.

I hadn't the strength to push him away. I turned
to him in sudden eagerness. He might know. "Can
I swim?" I asked.

"Like a mermaid," Mike said.

"Do you remember me drowning?"

Mike rocked back on his heels, surprised. "Of
course I remember."

"Tell me." I gripped his hands.

Mike looked down at my hands holding his,
then back up. "Why? What happened just now?"

He wasn't going to say anything until I
explained so I did so, tersely, "Whenever I start to
remember something about my past I flash onto a
memory of drowning." *Murky water . . .* "But I
don't know when or how it happened."

"Actually," Mike said, "you drowned twice that I
know of."

I fastened my gaze on him, demanding with my
eyes.

"The first time doesn't really count. You were
mad at me for throwing you in the pool so you pretended you were drowning to make me feel bad."
Mike grinned. "I resuscitated you."

"You kissed me," I accused, the strange flash of

memory I'd had in the Induction chamber now explained. But that memory had nothing to do with the drowning memory of falling through dark green water. "What about the second time?" I asked.

Mike's smile vanished. "That was more serious. Dr. Frankenstein shot you, and you fell off the diving tower. You played dead to fool him, but the loss of blood made you so weak you almost drowned for real."

I frowned. I remembered falling, but through water, not from a tower. I couldn't remember being wounded. And the water I remembered had been cold, not warm, and stagnant, not chlorinated.

On the other hand, how many times could one person almost drown?

Mike changed the subject. "There's something you should know. I checked up on what Eddy told Timothy. Eddy's troubles with the law weren't just teenage pranks. He was accused of manslaughter. He had a fight with his girlfriend and abandoned her in a deserted place. It was dark and she was drunk; she walked off a cliff and died."

I felt chilled, but I wasn't surprised. "Was that all?"

Mike looked disappointed by my lack of response. "Do you really want to work for someone like that?"

I didn't see that I had much choice. I shrugged.

"I also did a computer search on Anaximander, but guess what? The only reference I turned up was to some dead Greek philosopher. According to the vital statistics database, the only Anaximander living today is a ten-month-old baby."

I was disturbed but hid it. "So? Anaximander must be an alias, that's all. I'm going upstairs. Good night."

Out of the corner of my eye I saw movement and instinctively threw up one arm. The medipatch in Mike's hand that he'd been about to slap onto my neck went flying.

Mike didn't hesitate. With his first plan shot, he immediately proceeded to plan B and tackled me to the floor. My breath whooshed out of me, and I felt the cold metal of a handcuff fasten around one wrist.

"Sorry, Angel," Mike breathed near my ear. "But this is for your own good." He slapped a sticky-gag over my mouth.

CHAPTER

13

MIKE WAS MY ENEMY. I cursed myself bitterly—what had I done when I interrupted his Loyalty Induction?

Even as the thought went through my head, I fought back, getting my knees up between Mike and me and kicking. He grunted as my knee caught him in the chest, and I twisted free.

I rolled to my feet, and my leg swept out in a karate kick. I aimed for Mike's chest, but he anticipated me and grabbed my ankle. He yanked. I lost my balance, and my upper body flew backward toward the floor. I got my hands under me as if I were doing a handspring and pushed off. I tried to do a scissor kick in Mike's face, but my heels thumped against his shoulder instead.

He hung on to my foot. "The Orphanage fire."

The words meant something to me. I remembered flames, and then the drowning memory kicked in. *Falling through cold water, my boots pulling me down—*

By the time I fought my way out of the memory, Mike had cuffed both my wrists together behind my back and had moved on to my feet.

His full body weight lay on my legs, preventing me from kicking, so I threw my body from side to side, trying to make a noise loud enough to attract the attention of the people upstairs. All I succeeded in doing was banging my head against a chair leg.

Within seconds Mike won the lopsided battle. I was immobilized, hands and feet tied, mouth gagged. I lay for a moment, breathing rapidly through my nose, saving strength for my next chance.

Always assuming I got another chance. What was Mike planning to do? Rob the house for the money he needed, or worse, kidnap Timothy again?

"Your Loyalty chip doesn't want you to remember me," Mike said, surprising me. His face was so close to mine that his breath washed my face. "It's using negative reinforcement to encourage you not to remember. Every time you start to remember something, the Loyalty chip uploads an unpleasant memory into your brain and you drown. I'm going to overload the chip's circuit and break the pattern. *The Orphanage fire.*"

I started to remember again, orange flames licking inside my mind, and then the water came, drowning me. But when it was over Mike just triggered it again. "A group of radicals set fire to the Orphanage where the violet-eyed children were being kept—" He kept talking, reciting my life. He didn't give me any respite from the memories, but there was tenderness in the way he hauled me up, dripping, from the depths, one memory richer, before ruthlessly drowning me again.

"From the time you were three and I was four years old, we were brought up in the Historical Immersions of Canada in the 1970s and 1980s. We were told that it was the 1970s and 1980s, and we believed it. You and I lived in separate towns until 1987.

"We met down by the river. . . . Your best friend was Wendy Lindstrom. . . . Her boyfriend's name was Carl." Nudged by Mike's voice, the memories flooded back to me. I remembered Wendy. How could I have forgotten Wendy? So tough on the outside, so fragile within. The most loyal friend anybody could hope for. I'd missed her without even knowing whom I was missing.

Best of all, Mike gave me back my parents. Originally actors who had been hired by Dr. Frankenstein to play the part of being my parents, they had soon become my real parents. I loved them, and a pang tore through me when I thought of them. I missed them, and they must be worried about me. . . .

Staring out the window at the falling snow on Christmas Eve. My first Christmas with Mike and the joy of making our own little traditions. And the sadness of my first Christmas without my parents.

"What is it?" Mike had asked. He'd put his arm around me and bent his head close to mine.

"I want—" I'd stopped, swallowed the lump in my throat, went on. "I want to phone my parents."

"You can't. Anaximander would backtrace the call." Mike gave me a small one-armed hug, sympa-

*thy in his eyes, but no real understanding. His actor-
parents had been horrors.*

"There must be some way."

"Even if we knew how, we couldn't chance it,"
Mike said. *"What's to stop your parents from telling
Anaximander or the authorities our whereabouts?"*

"They wouldn't do that," I snapped.

*"They took Dr. Frankenstein's pay," Mike remind-
ed me.*

*"Only because they wanted a family. They love
me. I know I can't phone them—" Even if I could
have risked Anaximander tracing the call, I didn't
know my parents' vidphone number or where
they lived. I wasn't even sure if their last name
was Eastland, or if that had just been part of the
role they had played for so long. "—but I miss
them."*

Mike also gave me back myself, building a
bridge between Shadow Angel and New Angel.

I drowned a hundred times that night, and Mike
revived me every time. And each time I opened my
eyes, gasping, and looked into his violet eyes, he
came into sharper and sharper focus. Not Michael
Vallant, accused thief, but Mike, my nemesis, my
rival, my partner, my boyfriend.

My other half.

"And you won the coin toss to get captured by
SilverDollar so we could try to get money and
identicards," Mike finished. He sounded tired. "If
we'd known about the Loyalty chips, we would
never have risked it. Do you believe me? Do you
remember me now?"

I was silent out of necessity.

"I guess there's only one way to find out," Mike

said grimly. He removed my gag and handcuffs and waited, his body as tense as a metal spring.

My throat was too choked with emotion to make talking easy so I kissed him in answer.

"Angel!" He kissed me back, his arms coming around me in an ecstatic hug. "I was afraid I'd lost you," he admitted a little while later. We were lying side by side on the carpet.

I shuddered. "I lost myself for a little while, but I'm back now."

Rage vibrated in Mike's voice. "I'm going to get those bastards for what they did to you. SilverDollar will pay. Before I'm done with them, they'll throw money at us just to make us go away."

Coldness shafted through my bones like an arrow. "Don't say that," I said urgently. "Take it back." Without permission, my hand stealthily reached out and picked up the Knockout medi-patch that Mike had dropped on the floor earlier.

Mike didn't notice.

"No." His voice was hard. "I thought what Dr. Frankenstein did to us was bad, but this . . . I'm going to smash them until there's nothing left but shards, and then I'm going to smash the shards, too."

"Shut up!" I was frantic now. "You can't say that!"

"Sure I can—" Mike stopped, suddenly wary. "What is it? If the room was bugged, Anaximander would have burst in and stopped me while I was breaking your memory block."

"There's no bug," I said, throat dry. "Just me." I fingered the medi-patch behind my back, peeled off the protective film.

Mike didn't get it.

"Tell me you were kidding," I said fiercely. "Tell me it was anger talking, that you didn't really threaten SilverDollar. Tell me!" My nails dug into my palms, still holding the Knockout patch.

After the briefest hesitation, Mike said soothingly, "I was just mouthing off. I didn't mean it. How could someone like me hurt a giant corporation like SilverDollar? It's ridiculous. I'd have to be crazy to even try."

I held my breath, seeing if his denial would work. No go. "You're lying," I said. There were tears on my cheeks as my Loyalty chip made me hit him with a Knockout patch.

The ten seconds until Mike lost consciousness were the longest in my life. The wounded look in his eyes . . .

I had betrayed Mike again. The thought hammered into me, even as I used his own handcuffs to attach him to a heavy piece of furniture.

The thought of what Eddy would do to him, force him to go through Induction all over again and install a working chip, made me want to retch. The consequences for me were hardly less scary—at the very least, my memory would be wiped again, and this time there would be no notes to bring back Shadow Angel—but I still found myself starting up the basement stairs to call Anaximander.

Helplessly, I watched my foot settle on the bottom stair step—

No! I grabbed my ankles and yanked. My feet kept moving, but the awkward bent-over position made me fall sideways against the wall.

There had to be a way out of this, a way to satisfy my chip and save Mike at the same time, if I could just think of it.

Against my will, I began to climb the stairs again, but more slowly, placing both feet on each step, my hands still holding my ankles. One step. Two. Three. I had to think quickly before it was too late.

I had foiled the chip once before. When I tried to release Mike it hadn't wanted me to, but I'd convinced myself and it that I wasn't being disloyal to SilverDollar, that I was trying to save SilverDollar from an overzealous employee.

Okay then. Perhaps Mike had only meant that he wanted to punish the person who had installed my Loyalty chip. I tested out the rationale, loosening my grip slightly.

I climbed two steps before I caught myself again. I was almost at the top of the stairs.

Obviously, that wasn't going to work; I no longer believed the chip had been installed without Eddy's full knowledge.

Nothing less than Mike swearing absolute loyalty to SilverDollar was going to satisfy my chip, and even then it probably wouldn't believe him.

Unless . . .

I released my ankles and went upstairs. I tiptoed into the bedroom Rianne and I shared—she kept sleeping, thankfully—and took out a small kit from a hidden compartment in my palmtop's carrying case.

Mike had regained consciousness by the time I got back. I turned the lights on, set to low. The stony look on his face made me close my eyes against tears.

"I'm sorry," I apologized helplessly. "The Loyalty chip is making me do this."

The accusation in his eyes lightened but did not totally disappear. I winced. Mike had never trusted easily, and now I had betrayed him twice.

"The only way the chip will let me release you is if you swear that you'll be a loyal SilverDollar employee from now on. You have to," I said fiercely, "it's our only chance."

"I swear I'll be a loyal employee from now on," Mike said.

I could read nothing from his face, his expression opaque. "The words alone aren't good enough. You have to mean it."

Mike watched warily, as I ripped open the plastic pack of medi-patches soaked with TrueFalse and pulled off the plastic film. "What's that?" he asked.

"TrueFalse, a truth serum." I paused. "Didn't Anaximander interrogate you this way when you were first captured?" I had a vague memory of TrueFalse being used on me during my Loyalty Induction, but the Induction, my missing angel pendant, and the drowning were the sole bits of my memory that had not fully returned.

"No."

Anaximander had lied to keep me out of the way.

But that wasn't important now. "You have to change your mind," I told Mike. My eyes pleaded with him as my hands competently stuck the patch on his neck right over the carotid artery for faster absorption.

"I'm mad at what SilverDollar did, but since you

have your memory back I guess I can set aside my revenge. If losing you is the alternative, I swear I'll be a loyal employee," Mike said softly. "SilverDollar is probably no worse than any other employer."

I believed he meant the last statement but not the rest.

Four minutes ticked by.

Mike stirred restlessly. "You fought it once, Angel. Can't you fight it again? Just for a little while? Long enough to free me? I'll take it from there."

I tried. God help me, I tried to make my hands move to unlock his handcuffs until sweat stood out on my forehead and only thirty seconds remained on the clock. Gasping, I gave in. "I can't. I can't, I can't, I can't. Please, Mike," I was begging him. "This is the only way. Change your mind."

His lips tightened, and he looked away.

"Refusing to talk won't help you," I told him. "TrueFalse was designed to prevent spies from being tortured for information; it also loosens the tongue." *As he would soon find out.* "Time's up," I said hopelessly. "Swear or the chip will make me call Anaximander right now."

Mike swore viciously. "Only for you, Angel. I swear I'll be a loyal employee."

When a person lied under TrueFalse, they started to sweat. Mike's forehead remained dry.

I wasn't fooled. "I swear I'll be a loyal employee *to SilverDollar.*"

"I swear I'll be a loyal employee to SilverDollar," Mike recited obediently.

No sweat. Frowning, I reached out and touched his skin. It was dry.

I still didn't believe him. What was I missing?

Got it. "I swear I'll be a loyal employee to SilverDollar from now on."

Mike balked. "And if they fire me, what do I do? Commit hara-kiri?"

I hastily revised the oath. "I swear I'll be a loyal employee to SilverDollar, and even after I no longer work for them, I will not do anything to harm them."

Mike bared his teeth, but he repeated the oath successfully. No sweat. He was telling the truth.

The sudden release of tension left me almost boneless. "Thank God."

"Now that my loyalty is assured, do you think you could untie me?" Mike asked sourly.

"Sorry." I jumped up and unfastened his handcuffs.

Mike rubbed his wrists. "Exactly how long do the effects of TrueFalse last anyhow?"

"For ten hours or until I give you the antidote." I took out the second plastic package and gave him the antidote patch. "It'll take another ten minutes to take effect. Until then, you'll still have to tell the truth."

"Swell." Mike leaned against the wall, eyes closed. "Anything else you wanted to ask me?" he asked sarcastically.

Do you still love me? I pressed my lips together on that painful question.

My silence must have been telling. Mike opened his eyes. "Come on, Angel. This is your chance. Ask."

I phrased my response carefully, not sure I could take his answer. "If I were to ask you something, I would ask: Can you forgive me?"

Mike reached out and took my cold hand. "Of course."

His answer should have made me feel better, but it didn't. Dismally, I realized that I could not forgive myself.

"Where've you been?" Rianne demanded when I returned to our room. She had awakened in my absence and been surprised to find I had not yet come to bed.

"Talking with Mike."

"Talking?" Rianne sounded skeptical.

I went on the attack. "Yes. So what's with you and Timothy? You were one hundred percent flirting with him tonight. Did you decide that you like him after all?"

"Of course not," Rianne said shortly. "I was just having fun."

I said nothing, but I didn't believe her.

Rianne must not have believed herself either, because three minutes later she whispered, "How can you like someone and hate him at the same time?"

I remembered the rivalry that had sparked between Mike and me the first time I'd met him in 1987. "That happened to me once. I found out later that I didn't hate him at all, that I'd just thrown up reasons not to like him because I was scared by *how much* I liked him."

I rather thought something similar had happened with Rianne. She was so certain that no rich boy was going to fall for a poor disabled girl that she'd sabotaged any possible relationship from the very beginning.

CHAPTER

14

I STARED AT THE DOOR in frustration. On the other side lay freedom, but I couldn't get to it.

I'd spent the past hour trying to break my Loyalty chip—and failing. I'd tried running at the door to see if momentum would sweep me past the threshold. I'd tried sneaking up on it, pretending that all I was going to do was walk past and then suddenly veering sideways. I'd tried breaking down the task into little steps, first opening the door and then standing on the porch.

And here I still was in the front hall. The instant I thought about escaping, my muscles froze up.

It was almost time for breakfast. One more try and then I'd give up, I promised myself.

Reciting tongue twisters in my head while making my attempt didn't work either. But I couldn't give up.

Mad at myself and the chip, I gave up finesse and threw all my furious energy into turning my body toward the exit. I began to breathe as if I was a long distance runner, my face turning red, but my shoes didn't move, as if stuck to the floor.

Mike found me there in the hall. "Angel?" His face showed concern.

"I'm going to do it this time," I puffed.

He let me try for another thirty seconds before roughly pulling me inside his bedroom. "You have to stop doing that. You'll hurt yourself."

"I don't care," I said between clenched teeth.

"Well, I do. You just got your memory back last night. Be patient."

He was right. "Whoever genetically engineered me forgot to splice in the patience gene," I said wryly. "But I'll try."

"Good. Let's go to breakfast."

Graciana caught us in the hall. "A phone call for Miss Angel."

Anaximander? I wondered as I went to the living room. Eddy? Please no. Whoever it was, it wouldn't be whom I most hoped to hear from: my parents.

I pressed the vidphone Accept button, and the blank screen in front of me jumped into focus. It was President Castellan again, live this time, from an aircar.

"Angel, I just heard about what happened with the reporter yesterday. I'd like to thank you for your quick thinking."

"It was nothing," I said, pleased. Anaximander could take lessons from her. "I just wish I could have stopped Seth altogether. Has the story broken?" I asked.

"Not yet." She looked grim. "I think they're waiting until the awards ceremony this morning. Timothy will be there to present the awards. He's

worked so hard on this symposium, today should
be his triumph." Anger and frustration thickened
her voice. "And now it's going to be ruined. I've
tried to persuade Timothy not to attend the pres-
entation, but he's insistent."

"Will you be there?" I asked. Timothy would
need the support. It was eight o'clock; the awards
were scheduled to begin at nine thirty.

"Come hell or high water. Whether Timothy
wants me there or not."

"Of course, he wants you here," I said, feeling
somewhat bemused. Yesterday I'd reassured the
son, today the mother.

"I wish that were true." President Castellan's
eyes lost focus. "He blames me for not getting him
home sooner."

"From his kidnapping, you mean?"

"Yes. Those *robots*," she said, meaning the
Spacers. "I paid the first ransom too fast. I should
have negotiated. Eddy recommended it, and for
once in his sorry life he was right. I was desperate
to get Timothy back so I paid the million the
Spacers demanded without a fuss. And then they
got greedy. They kept asking for more and more. I
bankrupted my savings.

"And then"—President Castellan looked, if possible, even more incensed—"that cockroach who
calls himself my half-brother, that bungler, went
behind my back to the board of directors and
called for my resignation. He tried to get himself
appointed president in my place on the grounds
that Timothy's kidnapping had rendered my judg-
ment 'unsound.' He all but accused me of paying
the ransom with SilverDollar's money."

"What did Eddy bungle?" I asked.

"It would be easier to say what he hasn't bungled, which is nothing," President Castellan said acidly. "I'll never forgive him for the way he handled Timothy's kidnapping, delay after delay after delay. We finally get the Spacers to agree to send a negotiator and what happens? She has a heart attack and dies within a day. Why didn't he have medical staff on hand if she had a heart condition?" the president seethed.

"And now I'm stuck with Eddy. The board reversed my decision to fire him, saying it was in retaliation for his attempt to get me removed from office."

"Does Timothy know any of this?"

She shook her head. "No. If I say anything against his uncle Eddy, he gets mad at me."

I felt sorry for Timothy's mother and decided to give her a hint. "I realize you probably didn't want to worry Timothy with money problems or make him feel guilty about the size of the ransom you paid for him, but you might want to mention your money shortage to Timothy. He's laboring under the impression that the negotiations dragged on because you refused to pay. He thinks Eddy rescued him."

"What!" Outrage radiated from her face and voice before she clamped down. "Excuse me, Angel. I have some calls to make." The screen reverted to the main menu.

I smiled. President Castellan had the look of a woman who was going to right an injustice. *Take that, Eddy*.

Eddy was almost certainly behind the Loyalty

chip scheme. Anaximander would, of necessity, be in on it, too, but I felt no desire to get revenge on him. I was almost positive that Anaximander also had a Loyalty chip. I remembered the way he'd staggered after looking at Eddy's strange butterfly necklace. He'd looked the way I felt when I was trying to remember something and the drowning memory slammed into me.

Eddy should pay for that crime, too.

And then it hit me, a thought so beautiful and so simple that it made me dizzy: President Castellan might not know about the Loyalty chips. Eddy might have been acting on his own, illegally. He was Head of Operations, with a lot of authority of his own, and he had the magic Castellan last name. His subordinates would assume that the president knew. During the long months of Timothy's kidnapping, President Castellan's control of her company had slipped, and the Taber facility where the Inductions had taken place was located far away from Tucson. She truly might not know.

If Mike and I told President Castellan for the good of the company, my chip wouldn't object. We would be free.

I went to find Mike to tell him, but he wasn't in the dining room, or the bathroom, or anywhere in the house.

Alarm jumped inside me. I could think of no good reason for him to have left the house and several bad reasons.

One, he could be in trouble of some kind. Two, he could have slipped out for some clandestine reason while I was otherwise occupied. Three, he could have left, period.

It was possibility number three that scared me the most.

The reason I'd tried so hard to break free of the chip was because I was afraid Mike might decide that I was a lost cause and bail out. There were no strings on him.

I began to pace, deliberately thinking up innocuous reasons for Mike to have left the house: to get a breath of fresh air, to pick flowers for me.

I'd thought of fourteen lame reasons, when Mike breezed back in through the front door.

"Where were you?" I demanded.

"Angel." Mike smiled at me; his violet eyes lit with warmth. "Did you miss me?" He kissed me.

I kissed him back but wasn't distracted. "Where were you?"

"We shouldn't talk here," Mike said. We stepped into his empty bedroom. "I wanted to talk to Anaximander about the security arrangements he's made to protect Timothy from reporters. Unfortunately, I couldn't find him."

It sounded logical, but I felt a small thrill. If his absence had been so simple he would have waited until I was off the vidphone and either told me what he was doing or invited me along. He was hiding something from me, something he didn't want my chip to know. *Had he found a way around my chip?*

I tried to keep the thought from my Loyalty chip by thinking hard about who would win the essay contest.

God help me, I tried, but the chip caught the thread of guilt and began to chew at my mind. It worried at the question like a buzzing dragonfly trapped in my skull, creating a weird dissonance that dropped me to my knees.

I vomited.

Mike was at my side in a flash. "Angel?"

I swallowed down bile. "You're hiding something from me. What is it?" In another moment the chip would make me bring out the TrueFalse again.

"I wanted to wait until I had proof, impress you," Mike said quickly. "I think Seth Lopez is a Spacer."

Whatever I had been expecting it wasn't that. "What?"

"I don't think he's a reporter. I did a computer search and couldn't turn up any bylines or credits for that name."

My nausea faded. "What did you find?"

"Nothing. Five Seth Lopezes in the database, none of them listed as having silver eyes. I think he may have been trying to get close enough to Timothy to kidnap him again."

A tide of relief washed through me. *Mike hadn't been plotting against SilverDollar.*

I wouldn't have to betray him again.

"So who called you anyhow?" Mike asked after I'd freshened up and we'd cleaned the floor.

I told him about my conversation with Timothy's mother and my hope that she was unaware of the illegal Loyalty chip Eddy had installed. With luck, she would seize the excuse to fire Eddy, and my chip would be removed.

Mike shook his head. "It's too risky. What if she's in on the plan? Or even if she isn't, she may decide to neutralize us rather than let the UN find out and penalize SilverDollar."

My face fell. He was right. And now that he'd pointed out the danger to SilverDollar's reputation, my Loyalty chip wouldn't let me pursue any avenues that led to the UN finding out. Arrgh.

Everything led back to the chip. I was stuck in an endless loop.

"Why are you still here?" I whispered, tears in my eyes. "Why haven't you given up on me?"

I expected—hoped—that Mike would say something reassuring, like, I love you, or, I'll never leave you. "I can't," he said, and then, terrifyingly, he added, "Not yet."

Yet. My heart thudded. He planned to leave me. Just not yet.

He went on, the words obviously painful to him. "You'd fight forever for me, but I'm not as strong as you are, Angel."

Strong? I wondered bitterly how he could call me strong when I couldn't even defeat one microchip. The thought of Mike leaving me behind frightened me. I'd only just found him again. Words deserted me. I reached up and kissed him. Mike's arms closed around me with equal desperation.

"There's a voice inside my head that says, Cut and run, grab your freedom while you can. But if I go, I'll be alone again. I was alone from the time of the Orphanage fire until I met you last year. You're the only one who knows me, Angel," Mike confessed. "The only one who *can* know me. With everyone else I'm just playing a part. If I have to, I'll leave and be alone again, but I don't want to."

I hugged him harder, feeling the strong bones in

his back. I knew how difficult it was for him to say what he was feeling. I wanted to tell him that I loved him, but right now the words would only make him feel guiltier.

"We'd better grab some breakfast," Mike said finally, kissing me on the forehead.

I nodded, reluctantly unpeeling myself from him.

Dahlia was speaking as we entered the dining room. "Three of our trustees are coming to see which one of us wins."

Rianne bristled. "How nice for you. What if neither of you wins? There are three other finalists, you know."

Dahlia sniffed to show how unlikely she thought that was.

"Do you know your trustees well?" I asked Dahlia as I helped myself to some toast and jam. "Are they sort of like unofficial aunts and uncles?"

"Of course not," Dahlia said scornfully. "They've always known that they would have to choose between me and Zinnia, so they've been careful not to get too personally involved."

It sounded like a cold way to be raised to me. "What about grandparents?" I asked. "Iris Cartwright's parents. I guess, technically, they're your parents, too. Are they coming?"

"We've never met them," Zinnia said sadly.

"Why not?" I asked.

Dahlia answered me. "They disapproved of Iris's decision to have herself cloned. They actually went to court to try to get custody over us using the very same argument. The trustees won, of course. We're not their children; we're Iris's clones. You'd

think the difference would be obvious." Dahlia
rolled her eyes.

I privately thought she and Zinnia might well
have been better off being raised by Iris Cartwright's
parents rather than trustees. "My parents can't
make it. What about you, Timothy?"

"My mother's going to present the award. She
has to be there." Timothy looked a little desperate.

A thought struck me. "And is your father coming?"

"Oh, no, my father's dead," Timothy said casually.

"I'm sorry," I said.

"It's okay." Timothy shrugged. "He died seven
years before I was born. I'm a Legacy baby."

Timothy seemed to find nothing unusual with
his statement. Neither did the clones or Rianne.
Only Mike and I were caught flat-footed. "What?" I
asked.

"Mom had his DNA on file," Timothy explained
politely, "and she never remarried. She said that,
even if she had, she would still have wanted to have
my dad's baby. I guess he was a pretty neat guy."
Timothy sighed. "I wish I could have met him."

While I could see the horrible temptation to
turn back the clock to keep part of a loved one
alive by bearing his child, the result was that
Timothy had never had a chance to have a father.
No wonder he hero-worshipped Eddy.

It made me feel odd and out of time. I could
and had learned a lot of the future technology
that made 2099 different from the time I'd been
raised in. I could fly an aircar, operate a vidphone, and use a palmtop computer. I could

study up on the history. But what kept slapping me in the face was the social change: Legacy children, clones, Augments.

After breakfast, Zinnia lingered to speak to Rianne. "I'm sorry Dahlia was rude to you."

"Dahlia's the one who owes me an apology," Rianne said.

"I know," Zinnia said. "I just wanted you guys to know that she didn't used to be like this. We used to be great friends." Zinnia looked wistful.

"We always planned to run Iris's company together. But on our sixteenth birthday we got into an argument about who would win the estate. I said that I would win because I did better in class than she did, but Dahlia got really quiet and said that that didn't mean she was stupid. Ever since then she's been determined to beat me. She's going to do it, too." Zinnia looked depressed. "I can feel it."

"If you ask me, the loser may be the real winner," I said bracingly. "A hundred doors will open for the one that closed. From then on you'll be able to do what you want, no more slaving away trying to prove yourself worthy of a dead woman. Companies will fall all over themselves to pay for your education and hire Iris Cartwright's clone."

But I'd misunderstood the reason that Zinnia was upset.

"I know I'll be able to get a job if I lose, but, whether I win or lose, I'll have to go on alone. Dahlia's been there my whole life; even when she's being horrid, she's still there. What will I do without her?"

I didn't know. The thought of being alone, without Mike, terrified me. I made my voice artificially bright. "Well, to start you can go to the awards ceremony with us."

Zinnia smiled weakly. "I guess I'll go get changed then."

"Me, too."

We all got dressed up and then drifted back into the living room until it was time to go.

Timothy became increasingly jittery as his mother didn't show. Mike finally got him out the door by pointing out that his mother might have decided to go straight from her aircar to the auditorium without stopping by the house.

"Don't worry," I told Timothy when we reached the auditorium and learned that President Castellan still hadn't arrived. "There will be a bunch of speeches, right? She's still got an hour before she needs to be here."

Timothy looked reassured. He disappeared backstage, and the five of us found seats together. Rianne parked her wheelchair in the aisle.

The first part of the ceremony—Best Exhibit, Most Creative Display, etc. for the Exhibition Hall—went well, if a little dully. There were news crews present, but no reporters jumped up to ask Timothy awkward questions.

But when it came time to announce the contest winner, Eddy came forward and said that President Castellan had been "unavoidably detained due to engine trouble" and that he would present the award on her behalf. Eddy seemed suspiciously well prepared, giving a long and rather unfunny speech. Timothy looked miserable as he handed Eddy the envelope.

"And the winner is . . ." Eddy paused an unnecessarily long time. "Zinnia Cartwright."

I'd been rather hoping Rianne would win—not just so she would get the money she needed, but so that the Cartwright clones' relationship wouldn't be damaged further—but I clapped hard.

Zinnia cast one agonized glance at Dahlia's white face—Dahlia's hands stayed in her lap—and then stood up.

But before Zinnia could make her way down the aisle to the stage, twenty men dressed in green camouflage and carrying machine guns burst into the auditorium.

CHAPTER

15

MY FIRST INSTINCT was to duck and roll, but I checked the impulse. Everyone else had frozen in his or her seat. Movement would single me out of the crowd, not save me.

I willed Timothy to press his panic button, but he seemed petrified up on the stage with his uncle.

Where the hell were Anaximander and his security forces?

Hands raised but not looking the least bit frightened, Eddy stepped forward. "What's going on? Is this a joke?"

A burst of automatic weapons' fire into the air shut him up.

"Are you okay?" I whispered to Rianne. She looked tense. The stress couldn't be good for her heart.

"I'm fine," she whispered back.

We both quieted as one of the terrorists played the muzzle of his gun over our row.

"Remain where you are!" a terrorist bellowed.

"Anyone who is standing will immediately sit down! Anyone who attacks us or tries to escape will be shot! If you all obey, no one will get hurt!"

Zinnia sat down in the aisle with all the grace of a table collapsing.

No one else moved. No one tried to play hero. I let out a sigh of relief—and then Eddy spoke. "Who are you?" He was too stupid to be afraid.

The terrorists didn't shoot him dead. A tall, capable-looking woman even answered his question, though she addressed the cameras, not Eddy.

"We are the Sons and Daughters of the Stars. We are here to protest the unconscionable closing of the Martian mines by the SilverDollar Mining Company. They will lay off thousands of our brethren, the Spacers, in their ruthless quest for money and power. We demand that the UN intervene. We demand that the mines and the path to the stars remain open."

"That's not true. SilverDollar has not yet made the decision to shut down the mines," Eddy said, confirming even as he denied.

A machine gun jabbed him in the belly. Eddy looked offended.

Some of the terrorists began to sift through the crowd, selecting hostages. It occurred to me that it was just as well that President Castellan had been detained.

I had expected Eddy to be taken hostage, but the terrorists must not have known who he was because they passed him over. They didn't pass over Timothy.

I exchanged glances with Mike. Should we make a move? He shook his head. *No.*

Timothy looked sick. I had a bad moment when I thought he might try to fight them, but his shoulders slumped in despair instead.

I clutched the arms of my chair to keep from leaping up. I told my chip over and over that there was nothing I could do against machine guns except die. That I was more valuable on the loose, organizing a rescue.

They took Zinnia. Tears rolled down her cheeks as she looked back over her shoulder at us. Dahlia let out a keening cry of distress, but Mike hushed her, shaking his head in warning.

Then the terrorist who'd given the order for everyone to remain seated reached our row. He passed over Dahlia but pointed his gun at Mike. "You."

I fought to keep still. The terrorist probably thought I was breathing hard out of fear, not suppressed action. He passed me over. . . .

And picked Rianne.

Rianne, with her stick legs and weak heart.

"You. Go to the front with the others."

Slowly, face pale, Rianne began to roll forward.

She might have a heart attack and die. I couldn't let it happen. "Take me," I said. "Her wheelchair will take up extra room and slow you down. Her family doesn't have any money to pay ransom. If they did, she would be Augmented."

Rianne shot me an angry look, mad at her weakness being made public. I didn't care. "Take me," I repeated, standing.

Four machine guns snapped into line, aimed at my chest.

"I'll take whoever I want, kid. Sit down," the terrorist growled. Thick maroon stripes had been painted onto his face. Coupled with a nose ring, they made him look brutal and fierce.

The makeup also obscured his face. Wipe it away and three quarters of the people in the crowd wouldn't be able to identify him. I made a point of looking more closely. He had a barrel-chested body and long, muscular arms. His hair was buzzed short, and his brown eyes were deep-set.

"I said, *sit down.*"

I put my hands on my hips, acting utterly fearless. "Not her, you idiot. Me! You're supposed to take me."

It worked. He scowled. "But—"

"And now you've made me blow my cover," I said irritably. I dared not glance down to see how Rianne and Dahlia were reacting to my pack of lies. "Do you know how much trouble it was to get close to the SilverDiaper kid? And all for nothing. You screwed it up!"

The guy in the face paint looked angry, but not yet convinced. "I'm going to have to talk to Orange about this."

Yipes! But I didn't back down from my new role. "You do that," I said. "You tell him how you screwed up."

"I was told to take the girl with the bad legs," he said.

What? No time to think what that meant. I wanted badly to look at Rianne—was she a Daughter of the Stars? If she was, she could blow me out of the water. But Rianne stayed silent, and I let momentum pull me along.

"Then the message got mixed up, it was supposed to be the person *beside* the girl with bad legs," I said.

That seemed to do the trick. He glanced up at the front, where a group of hostages, including Mike, Zinnia, and Timothy, was already being hurried out the door. "We're holding things up. Let's go."

"Do you have a spare gun?" I asked. "Since my cover's blown, I might as well be of use."

"No. Not that I'd give you one anyway," the terrorist said as he backed up, covering the crowd with his machine gun.

Damn. I'd saved Rianne—if she had in fact needed saving, which I was beginning to suspect wasn't the case—but the longer this masquerade continued, the greater the chances of me giving myself away. As soon as we met up with this Orange guy, in fact.

"What's your code name?" the terrorist asked.

Orange could be a color or a fruit. "Lemon," I said. "And you?"

"Maroon."

Colors then. I should have guessed from his face paint.

We exited the auditorium, and Maroon broke into a run.

I had a chance to escape then. I could have fallen behind and sneaked back inside the auditorium, but not only did I not really want to explain to Anaximander that I had been merely pretending to be a terrorist, but continuing with the role gave me a slim chance of rescuing Timothy. The Loyalty chip didn't care just how slim that chance was.

The Sons and Daughters of the Stars were running a smooth operation. By the time Maroon and I reached the lawn where they'd landed their aircars, a fifteen-seater craft had lifted off and a second, smaller aircar was waiting for us with its doors open.

If I was going to do something, it had to be soon.

"Hey, Orange!" Maroon called. "I've got a bone to pick with you."

One of the men running in front of us turned back instead of entering the aircar. Seth Lopez.

Seth/Orange recognized me, too. "You!"

He was going to accuse me, so I accused him first. "That man's a traitor!"

The accusation, coming out of left field as it did, threw Seth. He sputtered a denial.

I watched Maroon. He was the important one. If he knew Seth/Orange well, my smoke screen would be blown away right here.

The gamble wasn't as great as it seemed. In an organization that used code names and disguises, members often knew well only the members of their own "cell" to protect the others in case of capture and interrogation.

My luck held. Maroon brought his gun up, pointing it at Seth.

"What are you doing?" Seth yelped. "Point that thing at her. I'm not a traitor, she is. She's not one of us! Where did you find her, anyway?"

"She's the special pickup *you* told me to get," Maroon said flatly.

"No, she's not! I said the one with bad legs." Seth glared at me.

"Which proves my point," I said smoothly. "He lied about the pickup; he's a traitor."

Maroon shifted his gun to cover us both. "I don't have time to sort this out now. Both of you get in the aircar. Move." Already the first aircar was almost out of sight, and the woman terrorist standing in the second aircar's hatch was gesturing frantically.

Seth went, swearing the whole way. "You're crazy!"

"Wise move," I complimented Maroon as I clambered inside the aircar. "The chase will be on any moment now."

Maroon scowled at us both. "Shut up and sit down."

I strapped myself in and looked around. *Damn it.* Timothy, Zinnia, and Mike weren't there; they must be in the other aircar.

"What's going on?" a woman asked. I recognized her as the terrorist who'd spoken so passionately to the cameras. She had a broad face with a large jaw. Long brown hair, tied back in a ponytail. Brown eyes. Crooked bottom teeth. From the stripes on her face, I assumed her code name was Blue.

"Later," Maroon said brusquely. "Go," he told the pilot.

The aircar lifted off with a screaming of engines. It occurred to me that Arizona Air Traffic Control didn't know our flight path, greatly increasing the risk of collision. Lovely.

Several tense minutes ticked by as we flew away from Tucson. We winged in the opposite direction of the first aircar, trying to draw pursuit. The tactic worked. A familiar Black Panther aircar buzzed after us: Anaximander. "Fall back or the hostages die," Maroon radioed. The Black Panther fell back without a shot being fired. We were alone in the sky.

The pursuit had been surprisingly easy to shake off. Almost suspiciously easy.

My heart bumped as I connected that fact with several others. One, Seth had escaped Anaximander before. Two, Anaximander was not incompetent. Three, Eddy hadn't been kidnapped. I added them up and threw in a couple of wild guesses to make five.

Eddy had wanted Timothy to be kidnapped. He'd either helped Seth or Seth was secretly working for Eddy.

I thought back to how Eddy had spoken of his nephew as being troubled and violent, and I felt cold. If I was right, Eddy was planning to kill Timothy and lay the blame on terrorists. I could see the scenario already: mentally unbalanced boy tries to escape his kidnappers and is shot dead.

At last I had the answer to why Eddy had placed Mike and me in Timothy's household. He would want our "loyal" testimony that Timothy was unstable. Both the locked planetarium incident and Seth's vicious questions had likely been planned to push Timothy over the edge.

Eddy had probably arranged to have President Castellan's aircar sabotaged to keep her from interfering.

Anaximander must be helping Eddy because of his Loyalty chip, because he had no choice. Just as I had no choice—

No! I breathed rapidly, making myself think

through the block. In a moment I found the chink. My loyalty was to SilverDollar, not Eddy himself. President Castellan was also part of SilverDollar. Timothy's murder would be another lever in Eddy's schemes to replace her as president.

I wrenched myself back to the present when Maroon returned from the cockpit to question Seth and me. "All right. Let's get to the bottom of this. Who are you?"

"I'm Orange. I don't know who the hell she is. Some meddler. What I'd like to know is how she came to be with *you*"—Seth skated on the edge of accusing Maroon—"and what happened to the girl you were supposed to pick up!"

Maroon eyed him contemptuously. "Your turn," he said to me.

"I'm Lemon," I said. "His name is Seth Lopez. He works for Eddy Castellan."

This time Seth didn't rush to protest for a telling two seconds. *Confirmation.*

"Save it." Maroon cut him off when he did start. "We'll know the truth in a moment. Blue, get the TrueFalse."

I winced inwardly. I'd forgotten about TrueFalse. Oh, well, nothing to do now but hope that the terrorists would be so distracted by Seth's confession that they would forget about little old me.

Yeah, right.

Luckily, Blue seemed to have taken a disliking to Seth. She gave him TrueFalse first. Seth spent the ten minutes while the drug took effect trying to convince her and the others that they were making a mistake. Maroon and Blue ignored him. In fact, all of the terrorists were ominously silent. Hostile.

Maroon started the interrogation. "What's your name?"

"Orange." Seth's brow remained clear of sweat.

"What are your other names?" Maroon asked.

"Esteban Domingo." Seth tried to stop there, but more names spilled from his lips. "Seth Lopez, Silas Thorn, Sam Patterson." No sweat so far.

Maroon abandoned that line of questioning. "Are you a traitor?" he asked bluntly.

"No." Still no sweat. Seth began to look cocky again.

"You need to be more specific," I said quietly. "If his loyalty is to Eddy or himself, then acting against the Sons and Daughters of the Stars doesn't make him a traitor."

Maroon shot me a hard look but took my suggestion. "Do you work for SilverDollar?"

"No." Still no sweat, but Seth looked nervous again.

The next question did it. "Are you loyal to the Sons and Daughters of the Stars?"

"Yes," Seth said, but this time he perspired.

The mood in the aircar took on an ugly tone.

Seth was panicked into speech. "I'm not opposed to your aims!"

No new beads of sweat.

"Wipe his forehead," Maroon said.

Blue swiped off the perspiration from Seth's earlier lie.

"Repeat what you just said," Maroon commanded.

Seth calmed slightly. "My aims and yours are the same."

Again, the TrueFalse serum confirmed that he was telling the truth.

"He's hedging his definitions again," I said softly. "Ask him what your mutual aim is."

"That's stupid," Blue said. "Everyone knows our aim is to take the human race to the stars to fulfill our Great Destiny."

I risked speaking again. "I don't think Seth believes in a Great Destiny."

The look Maroon gave me made me think I was pushing my luck, but he asked Seth my question. "What is your aim?"

"To hand Timothy Castellan over to the Spacers."

"Why do you want this?"

"So the Martian mines won't be closed down," Seth said nervously. Plump beads of sweat burst out of his pores, running down his face. He was lying.

Maroon's face turned to stone as Blue scrubbed the damning evidence from Seth's face. She wasn't gentle about it either. "If you lie to me again, I will gut you. *Why do you want the Spacers to have possession of Timothy Castellan?*"

Seth trembled. "So that SilverDollar has a legitimate reason to attack the Spacers."

Except for the aircar's engine, the silence was deafening.

Maroon rocked back on his heels, absorbing the knowledge that his organization had been used as a dupe to hurt the very group he had been trying to protect. His troops looked angry and devastated by turns. Blue was openly fingering her gun.

"Vermilion, radio the other aircar and tell them to abort the mission," Maroon ordered. "Tell them not to hand the hostage Timothy Castellan over to our Spacer brothers, and warn the Spacers of possible treachery."

A young man with wavy red lines on his face moved to the front of the aircar to make the call. He returned four minutes later with bad news. "The switch has already been made. We don't know how to contact the Spacers."

My heart dropped to my knees. Poor Timothy.

"You've got to let me go," I said. "I have to save him."

"Not yet," Maroon said. "Not until I know where your loyalties lie."

I went very still but didn't fight when Blue administered the dose of TrueFalse. I could feel the drug moving through my veins and didn't like the sensation. I had ten minutes to decide what to say and to think about what would happen if I gave the wrong answer.

"What's your name?" Maroon asked.

"Angel Eastland." I told the truth, hoping he wouldn't ask if my code name were Lemon.

He didn't. "Are you loyal to the Sons and Daughters of the Stars?"

"I am loyal neither to the Sons and Daughters of the Stars, nor to Eddy Castellan," I said calmly.

A ripple went through the watchers, but they didn't regard me with the same hostility they did Seth. So far, so good.

"Then what is your part in this?" Maroon asked, curious. "You are not just a student."

Quicksand opened up in front of me. If I told

them I worked for SilverDollar, they would regard me as their enemy.

I had been silent too long. Blue was looking at me with suspicion. And so, in desperation, I lied. "I'm older than I look. I've been investigating Eddy Castellan. I work for the UN."

I lied under TrueFalse—and did not sweat.

CHAPTER

16

"VIOLET EYES LIE." The meaning of the first message I'd found suddenly became clear.

When NorAm created the violet-eyed superchildren, one of the "improvements" they must have made was the ability to lie under TrueFalse. They had intended to use us as spies, and the ability to lie was a useful skill for a spy to have.

"If she's UN, she's a danger to us," Blue said, recalling me to the interrogation. "She can identify us." Blue avoided looking at me, a bad sign.

Time to speak up before Blue decided how to dispose of my dead body. "You're not the ones I'm after. My mission is to bring down Eddy Castellan; you're incidental. Let me go and I won't tell my employer any details about your operation."

"They can get a description out of her under TrueFalse." Blue continued to speak to Maroon and ignore me.

"That's not true," I said forcefully. "You forget: the UN has to abide by its own laws, and the law says the subject must give permission before TrueFalse testimony is allowed. I'll simply refuse."

My lack of sweat convinced Maroon. "Okay, we'll let you go."

"Thank you."

On Maroon's instructions, the pilot set the aircar down in a deserted area. "I'll radio your location to the UN," Maroon promised as he administered the TrueFalse antidote. "You will tell them we had no knowledge of SilverDollar's plan?"

"I will." I looked straight into his brown eyes and lied. I wished I could tell the UN the truth and hand the whole mess over to them, but my Loyalty chip stood in the way. Loyalty dictated that Eddy be quietly removed from his position of power in the company, not arrested. An arrest spelled embarrassment for SilverDollar. Embarrassment meant that public opinion of SilverDollar would sour and its stock would drop. Arresting Eddy could cost SilverDollar millions.

"Can I give you a piece of advice?" I asked. "This whole thing stinks. If you want to come out of it smelling better than SilverDollar, you should release the other hostages." The Cartwright trustees would pay for Zinnia, but I wasn't sure if Eddy would pay a ransom for Mike. I reminded myself that if Mike could escape Dr. Frankenstein he could escape from terrorists, too.

From the glances Maroon and Blue exchanged, I gathered that release wasn't likely. The Sons and Daughters of the Stars probably needed the money.

I lifted a hand in farewell and stepped out into the desert heat. The wind from the lifting aircar blew a tumbleweed into some cactus.

For the next fifteen minutes, I tried very hard not to think about my ability to lie under TrueFalse. I paced and tried to worry about other things, like what I would do stuck in the desert without water if Maroon didn't keep his word to radio the UN or the UN didn't send someone to pick up their "agent."

I tried and failed.

Next, I tried to convince myself (and therefore the chip) that, for some reason, Blue hadn't dosed me with truth serum. That there had been a factory error in the batch of TrueFalse that my medipatch came from. But I knew better.

The note I'd written to myself during my Loyalty Induction said it all: "Violet eyes lie." I must have been interrogated under TrueFalse and discovered my ability to lie sometime in that memory-smudged period between kissing Mike good-bye and waking up a loyal employee of SilverDollar.

Which meant that all the violet-eyed could lie, which meant that Mike could have lied when he swore loyalty to SilverDollar.

It didn't mean he had, just that he could have. Likely, he hadn't known he could lie so hadn't chanced it. Only. . . . Only I had told him about the message I'd found in my sock. In my mind's eye, I could see his violet eyes widening with understanding.

I could hear the passion in his voice as he spoke about getting revenge on SilverDollar: "I'm going to smash them until there's nothing left but shards."

Mike, I feared, was not going to settle for the pallid revenge of having President Castellan fire Eddy. Mike hadn't believed me when I'd suggested earlier that Eddy was solely to blame for our illegal chips.

Mike was a hostage. He should be safely out of commission until this was over, but I didn't trust him not to escape and muck things up. And if he tried to take down SilverDollar in order to save me, I was afraid of what my Loyalty chip might make me do.

I thought there was a very good chance President Castellan would free me from my Loyalty chip once I spoke to her. But in the meantime I was its slave.

I was still frantically trying to think my way out of the trap when an aircar with UN insignia landed near me and Dr. Hatcher got out.

I should have been surprised that Dr. Hatcher, the symposium presenter who'd talked to me about choosing a career, was a UN operative, but my mind was too occupied with doomsday scenarios for it to register as more than a blink. "Hello, Dr. Hatcher."

"Angel Eastland. Why am I not surprised?"

My eyes narrowed. What did he mean by that?

"The message said that the Sons and Daughters of the Stars were returning our operative to us. Can I assume they meant you?" Dr. Hatcher looked around, but I was patently alone in the desert scrub.

"A small fib," I said glibly.

"Ah," Dr. Hatcher said. I had the uneasy impression that he actually understood, but he didn't press it. "Dahlia Cartwright testified that you belonged to the terrorist group. Was that also incorrect?"

"That was a ploy to be taken along," I said. "I work for SilverDollar. You can question me under TrueFalse if you like."

"I could," Dr. Hatcher agreed. "But it wouldn't do any good, would it? It doesn't matter. I happen to believe you.

He knew who I was. What I was. "Just who are you anyway?" I asked.

"I'm a UN specialist in human genetic experiments. Whenever there's a violation, I'm called in."

I felt cold. "What were you doing at the symposium?"

"My presence at the symposium was purely coincidental—I'm interested in the idea of adapting humans for life on Mars."

"Then you haven't been hunting me?"

"No." Dr. Hatcher looked sad. "Though perhaps I should have been," he said cryptically. "A colleague mentioned your name in connection with the essay contest, and I recognized it and sought you out."

"And why are you here in the desert?"

Dr. Hatcher shrugged. "I was on the spot. A UN operative is on his way; when he arrives, he'll take over. Genetics are my field, not terrorists."

I tried to decide if I believed him or not.

"There's something I'd like to say," Dr. Hatcher said. "I've wanted to say it for a long time."

"What?"

"I'd like to apologize for your treatment at the hands of Dr. Frank."

Dr. Frank, whom Mike and I had nicknamed Dr. Frankenstein, who had tried to sell Mike and me to the highest bidder.

"Oh, is that an *official* apology?" I asked bitterly.

"No. A personal one." Dr. Hatcher's steady gaze made me feel ashamed of the dig. "I was a rookie when the Needham administration was busted, but I still remember how horrified everyone was by the plight of the violet-eyed children. Genetic manipulation is illegal, but you yourselves were innocent. You posed quite a dilemma for us."

Meaning, I surmised, that some of them had wanted to sterilize or even kill all the violet-eyed children as nonhumans.

"I'm sorry we didn't do better by you," Dr. Hatcher said. "We made a mistake in letting NorAm retain guardianship of you."

"I'm sorry, too." My face was stiff and unforgiving. An apology didn't erase the crime that had been committed against Mike and me.

Dr. Hatcher cleared his throat. "In your note you said that you would rather be friends than enemies."

He was referring to the note I had left with Dr. Frankenstein's body, a veiled warning that we would fight back if people continued to persecute us for belonging to a different subspecies. "We would rather be your friends than your enemies. Don't start a war you can't win."

"I would like to be your friend, Angel."

I looked away, unable to bear the kindness in his eyes. I found myself unaccountably close to tears.

And then he wrecked it all by adding, "Though I disapprove of the path you've chosen, working for SilverDollar as hired guns."

I'm not working for them by choice, I screamed

silently, but, of course, the chip prevented me from saying so out loud. "Why?" I said flippantly instead. "Spying is what we were bred for."

Dr. Hatcher looked sad. "Leona said you wouldn't follow anyone's drum but your own. I guess she was wrong."

I took the bait. "You know Leona?"

"Yes. I was able to assist her and her brother in locating someone. She's a remarkable young woman. She's planning to become a marine biologist, you know. She's not the only Renaissance child living a normal life, either. I also know an actress, a geneticist, a firefighter, and an accountant."

"Are you offering to help us? Put us in some kind of protection program?"

"Yes. And pay for whatever education you may desire."

He was offering exactly what Mike and I had gotten into this mess trying to obtain. It was too good to be true. "And what do you want in return?" I asked.

"Nothing."

I looked into his eyes and believed him. Then I had to look away because the chip wouldn't let me accept. "I'll consider it," I said. Even that made my tongue feel thick with disloyalty. "If you truly want to be my friend, give me the fastest aircar you have."

I was hoping he'd offer me a ride, but Dr. Hatcher humbled me. He gestured to the sleek craft he'd arrived in. "Will this one do?"

I accepted, and after radioing for another aircar to come and pick him up, he stepped back and let me climb into the pilot's seat. He didn't ask me where I was going or what I needed it for, an enormous act of trust that would probably cost him his job.

"Good-bye, Angel. I hope we meet again someday."

I started to shut the door, then hesitated, fighting with the chip. "My parents. Can you tell them that I'm alive and that I love them?"

"I'd be happy to. But wouldn't you rather call them yourself? If you give me a moment, I can get you their number."

The chip was screaming with urgency already. "I don't have time." My hands slammed the door, and I blocked off all thoughts of my parents and Dr. Hatcher's amazing offer. I donned the headset and started the engines, overriding the preflight checks.

"Please set course," the computer said.

"Quito, New Inca Republic," I told it. "Maximum speed."

The Spacers' power base was in space. They would want to get Timothy off-planet as soon as possible, which meant the beanstalk, which meant Quito.

The beanstalk was an incredibly tall, thin tower stretching 35,890 kilometers from Earth to space. Elevators in the beanstalk used pulleys and counterweights to transfer goods into space without having to burn up the huge amounts of fuel needed to boost rockets out of Earth's gravity.

The beanstalk had to be built along the equator so as to be in geostationary orbit with Earth, just like a satellite. The UN had chosen to build the beanstalk in Quito because the city was close to the equator and several miles above sea level.

While the aircar lifted off and flew under AutoPilot, I tried to place a call to President Castellan. All her calls, though, were being shunted to security—meaning Anaximander and Eddy. I hung up quickly.

The clock read 11:20 A.M.

It was a four-hour flight from Tucson, Arizona, to Quito, and the Spacers holding Timothy had at least half an hour's head start. I took the aircar off AutoPilot and used the override to break the speed limit. The aircar's UN identification kept Air Traffic Control from doing anything more than complain. When I got tired or hungry, I let AutoPilot spell me for fifteen-minute breaks while I drank bottled water and ate some doughnuts I found in a paper bag.

I wanted to call beanstalk security to tell them to watch for Timothy and his kidnappers, but I lacked the authority. Beanstalk security would want confirmation from Anaximander or Eddy, and my Loyalty chip insisted on handling things quietly, on not telling people about Eddy's guilt.

At 4:41 P.M. Central Standard Time, the clouds parted suddenly to reveal the city of Quito, formerly in Ecuador, now part of the New Inca Republic. Quito lay in a narrow valley on the lower slopes of the Pichincha volcanoes. On my left, I could see the beanstalk bisecting the blue sky. Like Jack's beanstalk it was very tall and thin, only it ended in a space station at the top instead of the Giant's garden.

The beanstalk rapidly grew into a solid pillar on

the horizon. Its great shadow stretched out for miles. The uneven ground and varied heights of the buildings made it appear to ripple, the world's largest sundial.

Because my aircar was marked UN, Traffic assigned me a primo parking spot close to a motorized walkway. At its base, the beanstalk was close to a kilometer in diameter in order to anchor the weight of the tower.

Before I disembarked, I searched the aircar. I scrounged up a uniform with UN insignia, handcuffs, and three Knockout medi-patches.

Once I passed through the security checkpoint, I began to scan the crowd around me for someone carrying a gun. I didn't want to shoot anyone, but the Spacers holding Timothy hostage weren't likely to hand him over to me if I just said please.

I followed an armed security employee down an Authorized Personnel Only hallway. My UN insignia allowed me to get close to her without arousing her suspicion. I pretended to be in a tearing hurry. As I passed her, I brushed her bare forearm. She didn't even notice me attach the Knockout patch. Ten seconds later I turned back and disarmed her unconscious body where it lay in the hall.

Before tucking the gun into the small of my back, I examined it. From a lecture of Anaximander's, I identified it as a "softgun." The gun itself was made of regular metal, but it fired special bullets that could damage flesh but not pierce walls—a necessity in the fragile environment of space.

Clock ticking in my head, I slipped back into

the crowd, praying that Timothy and his kidnappers had not yet arrived.

The beanstalk had three elevators: a large freight elevator, a passenger express elevator, and a VIP luxury elevator, which took a more leisurely trip up, slowing when requested so that the VIPs could look down on Earth from above.

So as not to be conspicuous, I joined a line of about thirty people waiting for the next passenger elevator to the top of the beanstalk. They stared at a rapidly descending red dot.

I searched the crowd for Timothy or Zinnia or anyone with silver eyes.

The elevator arrived. I stepped casually out of line, as if I was waiting for someone who hadn't yet arrived. Passengers disembarked through a door in the back of the elevator while more passengers entered from the front. The elevator consisted of a chain of five cars instead of just one. Once one car was filled, the next one slid up and was filled.

Even so, I judged that the chances of two or three people getting a car to themselves were zero. It would be virtually impossible to take a hostage up in one of the passenger cars without a bystander noticing something amiss.

Which meant the VIP elevator. It waited patiently, its sign reading Reserved.

A code was required to open the doors, but my borrowed UN insignia got me past it. I entered.

Most of the elevator was taken up by a large lounge with a transparent wall, a number of leather couches, and a small bar with drinks in squeezable bulbs instead of bottles and glasses.

The discreet metal railings and brackets on the walls, floor, and ceiling puzzled me until I remembered that the top of the beanstalk was a space station with zero-G conditions. The handles were for people to hold onto in the absence of gravity, and the brackets were to hold things in place—not so important going up, but vital on a trip down.

Sure enough, one of the digital displays along one wall counted down the decreasing gravity as well as the time to go to reach the top, and the speed and altitude of the elevator.

The second room was a conference room with table, swivel chairs, a smaller window, and various communication devices.

The third room was a lush bathroom done in peacock blue. Discreet instructions on what to do if you felt light-headed, nauseous, or claustrophobic were printed by the mirror.

All three rooms were empty. For lack of a better choice I hid in the bathroom.

Ten minutes later I heard the doors open. I longed to be able to see. Had Timothy and the Spacers entered or some innocent business executive? I heard a few taps and the sound of something being snapped into gravity brackets. Rianne's wheelchair?

I had my softgun out in case anyone went to the bathroom, but the door stayed safely shut.

"Walk carefully," a female voice said—Rianne. "Don't try anything. One touch of the poison patch on your skin and you're dead. Mike, secure Timothy to a wall."

Until I heard her voice I hadn't really believed it despite the "special pickup" Seth had ordered, but it was true. Tiny, disabled Rianne was a Spacer and a kidnapper. I shook my head. Bizarre.

No wonder she hadn't known how to deal with Timothy's crush on her.

"I don't understand." Timothy's voice had the heaviness of someone who had been betrayed again. "When I saw you just before they hit me with Knockout, I thought you were another hostage. Why are you doing this, Rianne? Are you a Daughter of the Stars?"

"No," Rianne said. "I'm a Spacer."

A beat. "How much ransom are you asking?"

"No money, just that SilverDollar sign its ownership of the Martian mines and space station over to us. You'll be free soon. Think of it as a holiday," Rianne said, voice brittle.

"What if they won't agree?" Timothy asked in a dead voice.

"They will if they know what's good for them," Rianne snapped.

I quietly opened the bathroom door and peeked around it. Timothy's hands were free, but his foot was cuffed to a wall bracket. Mike stood beside him, and Rianne gripped Timothy's arm, poison patch ready.

"Don't do this to me," Timothy begged Rianne in the same dead voice. "I can't take it again. Don't turn me over to them. I'd rather die."

The conviction in his freckled face made me shiver.

"Don't talk like that," Mike said sharply. "The Spacers won't hurt you. You might have to spend a few boring months playing VR games and watching TV, that's all."

Timothy shook his head. *No, no, no.* "The last time I was kidnapped I spent six months in a gray room with four silent movies and a solitaire card game that never let me win. Six months of never hearing another human voice. Six months of silence." He clutched his ears as if blocking out screams.

My heart chilled. Damn Eddy to hell for helping this happen. Determination grew inside me, unprompted by the chip. I could not allow Timothy to be held for ransom again.

"Food just appeared every morning. I stayed up several times to try to catch them—even just a glimpse of hands—but they always waited until I was asleep. That was when I realized they had cameras, that they were watching me."

I flinched. When Mike and I had grown up in the Historical Immersion Project there had been secret cameras watching us. Now I understood the sleeping bag and pillow in Timothy's closet and his dread of people looking at him.

"That's not going to happen this time," Mike said firmly. "You'll be free in a week at most."

Timothy shook his head. "This time won't be any different from last time. The negotiations will bog down. Rianne, please promise me something."

Rianne said nothing.

"Please hold me on Mars and not in space. It used to drive me crazy knowing that the only thing on the other side of the wall might be vacuum. That if I escaped I'd die. I used to fantasize that I was on Mars, even though I knew the ship hadn't accelerated for long enough to reach Mars."

Rianne looked uneasy. "What difference does it

make where you're held? Mars doesn't have a breathable atmosphere."

"I know. But I'd rather die on Mars. Please, Rianne." Timothy looked haunted, and I began to understand where Timothy's obsession with terraforming Mars had come from.

"Stop talking about dying." Mike looked freaked out. "Rianne, tell him he won't be isolated. Tell him he'll be held on Mars."

"He'll be treated with the same compassion SilverDollar treats the Spacers," Rianne said, defiance stamped on her face. She knew it wasn't the promise Mike had asked for.

Mike started to pin her down. "And what does that mean?"

Timothy interrupted. "Will you stay with me? Mike? Please?"

Mike flinched. "I can't."

"Why not?"

Mike opened and closed his mouth, searching for the right words.

"Because he's in on it," Rianne said cruelly. "He's not your friend, Timothy. He agreed to help me kidnap you for a price."

CHAPTER

17

TIMOTHY LOOKED AT MIKE with wounded eyes. "Is this true?"

In front of my eyes, Mike turned to stone. The process was subtle. I doubted that Timothy or Rianne saw it, but I recognized it. Mike was shutting down, entering survivor mode. "Yes." His voice was brutally casual, hiding his emotions. Mike turned to Rianne, while simultaneously moving out of reach of her poison patch. "Speaking of our deal, it's time you coughed up."

"Here they are." Rianne looked annoyed. "Two identicards, one for you and one for Angel—although why I should help her after the way she screwed me today I don't know. Now I don't have an alibi."

"You're just mad at her because you didn't figure out she worked for SilverDollar until I told you. You were starting to think of her as a friend," Mike said. "And the mess today was your fault. If you'd told me what you had planned, I would have made sure Angel didn't attend the awards ceremony."

"If she didn't know who I was, why did she pretend to be a Daughter of the Stars and steal my spot?" Rianne demanded. "It was an idiotic thing to do."

Steel infused Mike's voice. "She was trying to save you. You told her about your heart condition. What was she supposed to think would happen when gun-toting terrorists kidnapped you? The miracle of it is that her chip let her try to save you."

"I can save myself," Rianne said flatly.

Unexpectedly, Mike became amused. "I'm sure you can. Now, where's the rest of it?"

"You'll get no money from us," Rianne said viciously. "The Spacers are poor."

"But soon, thanks in part to me, you'll own a thriving mine," Mike said. "Never mind, the money was a bonus. Where are the operating instructions for the Loyalty chip?"

"Here." Rianne handed him a palmtop computer and a device that resembled a remote control. "Are you sure you wouldn't rather take Angel into space? We have qualified technicians who could remove her chip."

Oh, Mike. My heart melted. He was trying to save me.

Too bad it wasn't going to work.

"Not a chance," Mike sneered. "What's to stop your qualified technician from reprogramming Angel instead of freeing her? I may not want to work for SilverDollar, but I don't want to work for you, either."

I'd heard enough. It was time to make my move.

I stepped out of the bathroom, softgun in hand. "Drop it!" I yelled at Rianne.

She hesitated, then swore and let her poison patch fall to the floor. I kicked it away from her wheelchair, still covering both Mike and Rianne with my own weapon. "Both of you, against the wall." They backed up. "Timothy, I work for SilverDollar. You're safe."

Timothy said nothing, and I dared not spare a glance his way. With the poison patch out of the way, I wasn't very worried about Rianne; Mike was another matter.

He smiled at me and didn't back up. "It's about time you showed up, Angel. I was starting to get worried. You heard what Rianne said? She's a Spacer."

"I heard." I kept my softgun trained on him. "I also heard you selling out."

To my surprise, Mike grinned harder. "Pretend–ing to sell out. I told her you and I worked for SilverDollar and that if she paid me, I would give her inside information. She was supposed to tell me the Spacer plan to kidnap Timothy, but she was too clever for me."

Mike's mixture of lies and truth made me issue a dry laugh. "If that's true, why didn't you tell me and Anaximander that she wasn't just a student?"

"What makes you think I didn't tell Anaximander?" Mike asked. "I didn't tell you, because I wanted to impress you when we reversed the sting. Obviously, I made a mistake." Mike successfully danced around the edge of the volcano again.

I hadn't spoken with Anaximander recently.

Mike could be telling the truth. There was something else wrong with Mike's explanation, but I didn't allow myself time to think about it. I relaxed my grip on the softgun, no longer targeting Mike's leg.

"When did you figure out that Rianne was a Spacer?" I asked. "She has no Augments. What gave her away?"

"Her lack of Augments," Mike said. "She has no Augments, *but she needs them.*"

"Of course." I felt stupid for not having seen it myself. "And who less likely to attract suspicion than a girl in a wheelchair?" I glanced away from Mike and saw that Rianne looked furious. Timothy had his eyes closed, pretending he was somewhere else.

"Exactly," Mike said. "Now, would you mind putting the gun down? If you want, I'll swear under TrueFalse that I've acted loyally."

It was the exact wrong thing to say. My chip pinged. "It's no good," I told him. "The chip knows that the violet-eyed are immune to TrueFalse."

The chip, the chip, the chip, the chip. I hated it with a virulence that was silly considering it was an inanimate object. It should be the chip's programmers toward whom I directed my hatred—

—and that made me remember something else Shadow Angel had been trying to make me forget. Rianne had given Mike operational instructions for Loyalty chips. The money and identicards could be brushed off as a cover story to tell Rianne, but there was only one reason Mike could have requested the operating manual for my chip.

In trying to save me, Mike had damned himself.

"Don't move," I told Mike. "If you move I'll have to shoot you, and I don't want to."

Mike stilled, but his eyes watched me every second. "Don't do this, Angel. If you take me in alive, they'll install a Loyalty chip in my brain and erase our memories."

"They might not," I said. "I'm going to go to President Castellan. I don't think she knows about the chips. Even if she does, she may let us go in gratitude for saving Timothy. Eddy—"

Mike cut off my explanation. "It's too big a risk. Leave me free in case President Castellan betrays you. Let me go."

I believed as hard as I could that all Mike wanted was my freedom, not revenge on SilverDollar. It didn't work. "No go. I have to take you in."

Mike paused. "And if I'd rather die than be turned into a slave like you?"

My mouth dried. "I'll try to wound you, but I might miss. *Please don't make me shoot you*. There's a good chance Timothy's mother will listen to us. If you're dead . . ." I couldn't complete the sentence; it was too horrible to think about. "Cuff your hand to one of the brackets." I threw a pair of handcuffs at him.

He caught them but didn't put them on. "What if I don't believe you'll really shoot me?" Terrifyingly, Mike moved away from Rianne and Timothy, taking a step closer to me.

I backed up a step, gasping like a beached fish. "Stop it! I can't control the chip! It doesn't care if you're dead or alive. I'll shoot you!" My finger tightened on the trigger, taking up the slack.

"Will you?" Mike took another step.

Another step and my back hit the wall. "Don't move! If you love me, don't move. Don't make me kill you."

"You love me," Mike said softly. "You could never kill me. I trust you, Angel. I trust you to beat the chip." He came closer.

I couldn't stop myself from firing the softgun, but I stamped down hard on my instep, throwing off my aim enough that the bullet hit Mike in the arm, not the chest. He was bowled over backward. His hand clamped over his upper arm. Blood oozed between his fingers. He swore a blue streak but didn't scream.

"I told you the chip would make me do it," I wailed. My arms were still locked in front of me in a shooter's stance. My gaze flicked to Rianne, and her chair stopped moving.

"But you didn't." Mike lifted his hand to look at the wound. "I'm not even seriously injured. You just grazed me. You won against the chip."

"Oh, no, you don't," I said. "Don't even think of trying this again. I might—*might*—succeed in avoiding a kill shot a second time but never a third. And if I'm responsible for your death, poison will eat me up from the inside."

Mike looked into my eyes for a long moment, nodded, and clumsily cuffed himself to a second wall bracket beside Timothy.

Timothy continued to ignore Mike and the rest of us, staring off into space as if he were already in sensory deprivation. If I hadn't been so worried about Mike, I would have worried about Timothy.

I pointed the softgun at Rianne. "Bandage him up."

Rianne folded her arms. "Why should I? He double-crossed me."

"Do it!"

Rianne wheeled herself over to him and used the sleeve of Mike's shirt to make a crude bandage. I winced every time she jarred his wounded arm.

"Why didn't you drug me and tie me up earlier, when you had the chance?" I asked Mike bitterly. "You had days to try to find operating instructions for the chip and deprogram me."

"Arrogance," Mike admitted. "I didn't think there was any point in escaping until we had what we came for, the money and identicards."

"Okay," I said to Rianne. "Your turn—"

And that's where I made my mistake. I grabbed Rianne's arm, and she exploded into action.

While I'd been confronting Mike, the elevator had continued to travel up the beanstalk. We'd reached zero-G, and Rianne no longer needed her wheelchair. Her weak legs were more than sufficient to move, and Rianne was a Spacer, born to zero-G.

Rianne pushed off from her chair, shoving me with her. I was so startled at finding my feet leaving the ground that I didn't react quickly enough and she knocked the softgun out of my hand. It went spinning off through the air.

My reflexes kicked in, but they were gravity reflexes. I lashed out with my left foot, but without solid ground to push off from, the movement was slow and awkward. Rianne easily sideslipped my foot, and, in horror, I felt my momentum drive

me forward past her so that my next slashes cut
only air. I began to tumble. My hair haloed out
from my head in all directions like a dandelion
puff.

On one of my revolutions, I saw Rianne kick off
from the ceiling, neatly changing direction. The
economy of movement was beautiful to watch.

Although I was a quick learner, I didn't stand a
chance against someone who'd dealt with zero-G
all her life. My only hope was for Rianne to under-
estimate me. So, instead of executing a somersault
turn and pushing off the wall with my feet the way
a swimmer did at the end of a lap, I let myself
smack into the wall. The impact stung my palms. I
ignored the pain and grabbed one of the handrails.
Once anchored, I clung there, looking around
wildly, but making the amateur mistake of not
looking up.

One, I counted to myself, watching Rianne's
shadow strike from above like a hawk. *Two. Now!*

I held tight to the handrail and flung myself
sideways. Her foot touched down on the wall
beside my head, knees bending to give her a
greater push off; I released the handrail and
seized both her ankles. I held on like death as
she thrashed and kicked. In close fighting, the
advantage was mine since I was stronger than
she was.

Rianne pushed off the wall with her hands,
sending us into a spinning tumble. If she'd been
hoping to make me vomit, she was disappointed. I
narrowed my eyes and pinned Rianne's ankles
together. A moment of groping in my pocket and I
found the second pair of handcuffs I'd borrowed

from the UN aircar. I snapped one around her left
ankle before she realized what I was doing.

Rianne screeched in outrage. She pulled my
hair and tried to gouge my eyes but missed, putting a long scratch down my left cheek instead. I
caught her wrist and cuffed it to her foot, then
pushed away from her, out of range of her spitting
rage.

I spent the next three minutes carefully collecting the softgun and poison patch and stopping the
elevator. Once matters were in hand, I would send
the elevator back to the ground, away from the
space station.

I turned my attention back to Rianne. I
bounced in her direction and used the back of her
belt to tow her back down to the ground. I
wouldn't want her to fall if the gravity returned too
abruptly.

"I won't be taken in," Rianne said. The determination in her face was so great that I would have
bet on her against a hurricane. Just not against my
Loyalty chip.

"I'm sorry," I said, and meant it. But, I was
ashamed to realize, I also felt a surge of satisfaction at having captured her, at having won. I wondered if competitiveness had been bred into my
genes or if it was a particular fault of mine. "I'm
sorry," I repeated.

Rianne wasn't listening. Her breathing sounded
harsh, labored. "I won't let them torture me, as
they hurt my mother. I won't give the Castellans
the satisfaction."

I started to explain that no one was going to be
tortured, that President Castellan would clip Eddy's

wings, then stopped. Listened. Rianne's breathing *was* labored. *Her heart condition.*

Frantically, I searched for her vial of pills, but she wasn't wearing her necklace today. "Where are your pills?"

She didn't answer. Hectic red spots showed on her cheeks. Incredibly, she smiled even as she gasped for breath. She looked vindicated, as if things were going according to plan.

CHAPTER

18

RIANNE WAS DELIBERATELY giving herself a heart attack.

I was instantly furious with her. "Are you crazy? Stop it!"

She didn't listen.

I stopped digging through her pockets for her pills—she must have left them behind on purpose in case she was captured—and prepared to give her CPR. I dragged her over to the nearest flat surface, uncuffed her ankle, and recuffed her to a bracket to anchor her.

If she'd been faking, it would have been a wonderful opportunity for her to attack, but Rianne wasn't faking. Already her lips were turning blue. As I straightened her body, she stopped breathing altogether.

I felt for the pulse in her throat where her carotid artery should be beating. No pulse.

"Angel, call for help," Mike said urgently. "Start the elevator up again."

I couldn't. If beanstalk paramedics showed up, the whole kidnapping story would come out, and the chip would rather risk Rianne's death than the embarrassment of Eddy's corruption.

I opened my mouth to tell Mike so, but shame stalled the words on my tongue. I hated words like *couldn't*, hated the way my body had betrayed me. "There's no time," I said instead.

It was true. Rianne's body was completely limp. Her eyes were half open, unseeing and unblinking, her jaw slack. She looked as if she was dead already.

I put my fingers on Rianne's chest, feeling for her breastbone so I could find her heart two finger-widths above it—and couldn't find it.

I was first startled and then panicked. How could Rianne not have a breastbone? I yanked up her white T-shirt—modesty had no place in first aid—and found something even more bizarre. A piece of black plastic shaped roughly like a butterfly was superglued over her heart. In the center, between the wings, was a flap hiding a microzipper. Apparently, Rianne's heart had been operated on so often that the doctors had removed her breastbone and installed a trapdoor for easy access.

A terrible chill went through me when I saw it, but I didn't have time to think about where I'd seen that black butterfly shape before.

I started to double up my hands over her heart as I had on so many CPR dummies, then stopped, unsure how much pressure I needed to compress her heart. Without a breastbone to take some of the pressure, both hands would be overkill, so I tried using the heel of one palm. Her chest compressed two inches with every stroke the way it was supposed to, but the recoil almost sent me spinning away. I clung grimly to her hips with my knees.

I started counting under my breath, "One, two, three, four. . . ." I made fifteen compressions in ten seconds.

Then over to her mouth to keep her breathing. One hand under her neck to tilt up her chin and open the airway, the other hand pinching her nose closed. Two slow breaths in.

Back to her chest. Fifteen compressions.

Back to her mouth. Two breaths.

After the third cycle, I stopped and listened for a heartbeat. Nothing.

She was so pale, so still. My hands shook even as I forced them to do the work.

Fifteen compressions. Two breaths. Fifteen compressions. Two breaths. Fifteen compressions. Two breaths. Listen.

Nothing.

I needed all my energy to keep the cycle going, but inside I was swearing at Rianne. Why the hell had she done this?

I was determined that she wasn't going to die. I kept going for long minutes after my arms felt like cooked spaghetti. Panic spiraled higher inside me when I still couldn't feel her pulse. She was dead. Rianne was dead.

"Angel!"

I looked up, suddenly aware that Mike had been calling my name for some time now. My hand didn't stop compressing Rianne's chest.

"Angel, you need help. Toss me the handcuff keys so I can come help you." Mike looked desperate.

I wanted to. Tears of fear and frustration dripped

down my nose. "I can't." Two breaths for Rianne. It was hopeless. She was dead. Fifteen compressions.

Mike braced both feet against the wall and pulled on the bracket, but it didn't come loose. "If you don't trust me, trust Timothy," Mike shouted.

Timothy. I'd forgotten about him. I looked up and saw that he was no longer off in never-never land. His expression was alert.

"Let me help her," Timothy pleaded. "I promise I won't free Mike."

I nodded, relieved by the solution. I fumbled out the handcuff key, between compressions. "You'll have to catch it the first try," I told Timothy.

He paled but nodded and held out his hands.

I took a deep breath, aimed as well as I could and then let fly. Timothy caught it.

I didn't stop to watch him free himself as I bent over Rianne's lifeless body. My back ached, and my arms no longer felt as if they were attached to my body. Hope was dying.

"You keep her breathing, I'll do her heart," Timothy said.

I moved over gratefully, too tired even to acknowledge him.

Three cycles later Rianne's heartbeat came back, and her chest began to rise and fall on its own. Color returned, creeping under her black skin and taking away her corpselike pallor.

I drifted weightlessly, mind and body exhausted. I kept watching her, afraid that her recovery wouldn't last, but her breathing improved, growing less ragged.

She was going to live. We had done it.

"What are we going to do?" Timothy asked after

a long moment. He still held to the wall bracket that Rianne's body was cuffed to, anchoring himself. "As soon as she wakes up, she'll just give herself another heart attack."

"We'll have to keep her unconscious with Knockout until she's in custody." Even as I said it, I was uneasy. Knockout might be dangerous to someone recovering from a heart attack.

"I think we should let her go." Timothy looked troubled.

"We can't let her go." The chip saw her as a threat to SilverDollar. My helplessness made me angry, and I took it out on Timothy. "Why do you care if she goes to jail? She's never been anything but rude to you, and she kidnapped you."

"I don't know why I care." Timothy's voice was low. "I just do." And then he kicked off from the wall, directly toward me. As we collided he pressed a Knockout patch on my arm.

I immediately tore the patch off, flinging it away. I dug out my atomizer of antiKnockout and triggered the nozzle, but, in zero-G, the mist formed into tiny beads, which floated away, uninhaled. And then it was too late. I could feel the drug moving through my veins.

Timothy shouldn't have had Knockout patches on his person. While I had been battling with Rianne, Mike must have given one to Timothy and told him about my Loyalty chip.

Thank you, Mike, I thought as I sank into unconsciousness.

When I woke up, I was bound hand and foot. To my surprise, so was Rianne, although she was now lying on the couch under Timothy's jacket and Timothy's watchful eye. She looked exhausted and irritable. I watched her through the screen of my eyelashes, not wanting everyone to know I was awake and aware.

We were still in the elevator. The car was stopped but had been moved far enough down the beanstalk to restore partial gravity. I hoped no one else had booked the VIP elevator.

"You're crazy to try it without a trained technician," Rianne told Mike.

"I know I'm not a surgeon," Mike said. "I'm not going to try to remove the chip from her head. I'm just going to switch it from Operative mode to Passive mode. It'll have the same effect."

Rianne shook her head. "Even if you do deactivate her chip, chances are her mind will be so screwed up that she'll still be loyal to SilverDollar. She'll betray you at the first opportunity, and I'll be taken in."

"You don't know Angel," Mike said. "She almost fought free of the chip twice on her own. She's warped its purpose to serve her own."

Funny, it didn't seem that way to me. The way I remembered it, the chip had bent me to its will like a pretzel. Even now, I was surreptitiously testing my bonds to see if I could slip my hands free of the cuffs. No go.

"That's impossible," Rianne said. "A Loyalty chip is absolute."

"She did it," Mike said proudly. "She should have tied you up as soon as she took away your poison. Instead, she wasted time talking to me and then even made you bandage up that tiny scratch on my arm, all to give the elevator time to reach zero-G and give you a chance to win."

"Carelessness," Rianne said.

Mike shook his head. "Not Angel. It was deliberate. Somehow she kept the chip from thinking about zero-G."

Shadow Angel at work again.

"She's awake," Timothy said, standing up.

Mike came and crouched by my body. "You know what I'm planning to do?"

I nodded.

"It's likely to be painful," he said softly.

Rianne snorted. "*Likely* to be painful? Tell her the truth: it's going to burn like hell, and the chance for success is only forty percent."

I smiled into Mike's violet eyes and repeated the words he'd once said to me. "I trust you."

Mike smiled back at me and said, "Timothy, brace her head."

Timothy obediently knelt by my head, using his knees and hands to keep me steady. The chip wanted me to buck and fight, but I told it that if I did Mike might accidentally fry my brain and then no one would be able to warn President Castellan of Eddy's treachery.

Mike pointed the remote at my forehead and started tapping buttons. Each one sent a small shock of pain through my skull.

This isn't so bad, I told myself. *It hurt worse than this when Dr. Frankenstein shot me—* And then, abruptly, it got very bad, as if the chip burned red hot, searing my brain. I tried to twist away from the source of the pain, screaming.

Dimly overhead, I could hear Mike swearing as

Timothy's knees clamped down on my ears. Then the pain grew too huge, and I convulsed, chest arching up—

When I woke up for the second time, I had a fierce headache. An hour earlier, I would have described it as excruciating. After the pain of deactivating my Loyalty chip, the pounding took on the half-pleasant rhythms of an extremely loud rock concert. I swallowed thickly and tried to sit up.

Mike studied me anxiously. "Angel?"

I closed my eyes and nodded, meaning yes, I would live and yes, the chip was silent.

Mike folded my fingers around a glass of water, and I drank it gratefully. I swallowed the pain pill he gave me.

"Now that she's okay, let me go," Rianne demanded.

"We'll miss you, too," Mike said sarcastically. "Remember our deal. You go free, but so does Timothy."

She nodded agreement, and he got out the handcuff keys.

I put down the glass. "Wait," I said weakly.

Mike stopped. Rianne went rigid, no doubt ready to give herself another heart attack.

I held up a hand. "No, go ahead and free her. I just want to talk to her."

"About what?" Rianne shakily sat up. "Stop hovering," she told Timothy. "You saw me take my medicine."

"About Eddy Castellan. Our common enemy." I turned to look at Timothy, and the movement made my head throb. "I'm sorry to tell you this, but your uncle is not a very nice man."

Timothy shook his head and looked stubborn. "You're wrong. It couldn't have been Uncle Eddy who installed your Loyalty chip. Maybe it was Anaximander," he offered.

"It was Eddy." I searched for the words that would convince him. I had no proof, but I knew.

Mike helped me out. "Do you know why Eddy went to jail when he was your age? It wasn't for a misdemeanor. The charge was manslaughter, but it was closer to murder. I looked it up on the news database; you can, too." Mike gave Timothy the details.

"We don't know his side of the story," Timothy insisted when Mike finished. "There could be more to it than that."

"Will you listen to my side of the story?" I asked him.

"Okay." Timothy cracked his knuckles.

I described my meetings with Eddy and the way he had constantly belittled Anaximander. I spoke of my certainty that Anaximander also had a Loyalty chip because he sometimes swayed the way I did when coping with the drowning memory. I told Timothy how Eddy had spoken of Timothy as being unbalanced and possibly violent. I reminded Timothy that the terrorists had not taken Eddy who, as Head of Operations, was a better hostage than Timothy.

When I finished Timothy looked miserable and indecisive. "I don't know."

"There's more," I said. "But it's not my story to tell. Rianne, I need you to tell us about your parents."

"My parents?" Rianne looked surprised. "What do they have to do with anything?"

Mike raised a questioning eyebrow, too. He sat down on one of the sofas and held me against his chest. I was all too glad of the support. I felt as if I'd been through a war.

"Maybe nothing," I said. "But I have a hunch they're important. Tell me about them."

Still looking baffled, she started. "The last name I've been using is an alias. My parents' names were Alex and Francine Pelletier. Is that the sort of thing you wanted to know?"

"Yes," I said. "You told me once that your mother had a similar heart condition to yours and died of a bad shock. Today you said that SilverDollar tortured her. Which is true?"

Rianne's dark eyes fastened on Timothy. "Both. SilverDollar killed her. My father, too."

"How?"

"It was my fault," Rianne said, surprising me. "They died because of me. Because I was born like this." She gestured to her spindly legs and touched her heart. "The doctors said that without an Augmented heart my life expectancy was sixteen. When I turned fifteen and SilverDollar still hadn't delivered the Augments it had promised time after time, Dad joined the Radicals."

"But SilverDollar spends millions every year on Augments," Timothy objected.

"Liar!" Rianne's eyes flashed. "That's what SilverDollar always says, but it's a bald-faced lie! They spend the bare minimum. My father received a Memory Recorder because it was essential to his job, but they never gave him the silver eyes he needed. They patched and repatched my heart, always waiting until it was an emergency, and then spending the least amount of money possible instead of buying me an Augmented heart and being done with it."

"Stop!" I yelled, then winced when my head threatened to fall off. "Timothy, you'll get your turn later. Rianne, please continue. Your father joined the Radicals . . . ?"

"Yes." Rianne glowered once more at Timothy and then went on. "The Radicals were tired of hollow promises. They wanted action. So they decided to kidnap the son of SilverDollar's president to force her to give us what we'd been promised. They were successful, but my father was caught and killed during the operation."

"How did your dad die?" I held my breath.

"He drowned. He was leading the pursuit away from the others, and his boat tipped. He'd lived his whole life in Space; he'd never learned to swim, and he drowned."

I took a deep breath. "Where did he drown?"

Rianne was staring. "In a bayou in Louisiana."

I summoned up the drowning memory. *Dropping down, down through murky green water. My boots dragging me down while my arms flailed.*

A bayou, not a chlorine-clear swimming pool. Weight in my legs instead of a bullet hole in the shoulder. I hadn't been remembering the showdown with Dr. Frankenstein. The drowning memory had been implanted along with the Loyalty chip. All this time I had been remembering something that happened to Rianne's father, not to me.

"And your mother?" I asked.

"The ransom negotiations weren't going well. Mom thought that if SilverDollar's president could just see for herself how much the Augments were needed, she would be persuaded. So Mom went down to Earth to negotiate. Two days later she died of a heart attack.

"They said the strain of the extra gravity had stressed her heart too much, but I've been on Earth longer, and my heart's weaker than hers was. They lied. They must have frightened her or hurt her to cause the heart attack. But even if they didn't cause the attack, my mother shouldn't have died. Earth has medical resources we can't hope to touch in space. SilverDollar could have saved her life if they'd wanted to."

Timothy looked sick.

I had a flash of memory. *President Castellan accusing Eddy of incompetence for not having a doctor on hand.* I felt ill, too, but I had to ask. "If your mother had the same heart condition as you, does that mean she also had a trapdoor in her chest?"

"Yes." Rianne studied me narrowly.

"Was there a word inscribed on it? Your father's name, perhaps? Alex?"

"Yes." Rianne looked spooked. "How did you know?"

"I know, because I've seen it. Eddy wears it around his neck when he wants to taunt your father—Anaximander."

CHAPTER

19

SILENCE.

"What did you say?" Rianne asked, a dangerous glint in her eye.

"Anaximander is your father." Alexander, Anaximander. Eddy would have found the closeness between the two names amusing.

"My father is dead." Rianne brushed that matter aside. "What did you say Eddy wears around his neck?"

I turned to Timothy; Rianne wasn't the only one I needed to convince. "Have you seen it? When Eddy's with Anaximander, he pulls it out and strokes it."

Timothy's gray eyes widened. "Oh, God. I have seen it. A piece of black plastic on a cord—just like the one over your heart, Rianne. I asked him what it was once. He said it was his good luck charm."

"I think I'm going to be sick," Rianne said.

Fortunately, she wasn't, but several moments passed before she spoke again. "Anaximander can't be my father. I've seen him. I would have recognized him."

"Are you sure? What if he's been Augmented since you last saw him? Shaved his head, been given the silver eyes he needed, maybe had the shape of his face altered. . . . Couldn't Anaximander be your father?"

She was still shaking her head. I changed tack. "Did you actually see your father's body?"

"It was cremated before being shipped to space," Rianne said reluctantly. "But that doesn't mean anything. I'm telling you: my father is dead."

"No." I shook my head, compassion in my gaze. "I'm afraid he's not. Eddy did something much worse to him than kill him. He turned him into his own worst enemy." Another practical joke for Eddy to laugh at.

"He is not Anaximander! My dad would never have—"

"Would never have stood by and watched your mother die?" I finished when she broke off. "Would never have left you alone? Not half an hour ago my Loyalty chip almost made me kill Mike."

Mike spoke up. "I told you how SilverDollar erased Angel's memories. If she hadn't managed to leave herself some clues, she never would have remembered me, never would have been anything but a loyal employee."

"Whenever I started to remember, a feedback loop would kick in, throwing me into a memory of drowning. None of my own memories were negative enough, so they implanted someone else's memory—your father's memory from his Memory Recorder Augment."

Rianne was shaking her head. No.

"Eddy," I added bitterly, "would have thought it amusing to make your father watch your mother die." As he had insisted that I help Anaximander capture Mike. I remembered suddenly that Anaximander had tried to talk Eddy out of it.

Rianne was crying. I touched her shoulder, but she shrugged me off, and I didn't try again. She had been alone too long. Timothy stood by, looking helpless. Her tears lasted under a minute. When she looked up again, hatred was carved into her face. "How do we get him?"

"*We* can't," I said. "We need to call in help, either the UN or President Castellan. I might have an in with someone who works for the UN." I explained about Dr. Hatcher's apology and offer of help. "I think he meant it. He gave me his aircar."

"Probably so he could tail you to the beanstalk," Mike said cynically. "No. I'm not winning free of SilverDollar just to let the UN put a leash on us. So he apologized. So what? Where was he for the years we spent stuck in the past?"

I thought Mike was being paranoid, but I wasn't one hundred percent sure of Dr. Hatcher. Mike and I had thought we knew what we were doing when we allowed one of us to be captured by SilverDollar. We had been very wrong then, so I stayed silent.

"It doesn't matter," Timothy said. "If we go to the UN, they'll arrest Rianne for kidnapping."

I winced. I hadn't thought about that. "President Castellan it is, then."

Neither Mike nor Rianne was happy with that

decision, but they couldn't come up with a better idea.

"Timothy, I need you to call Graciana," I said. "Eddy's screening your mother's calls. If we try to phone her directly, the message will never get through."

Timothy agreed and went into the conference room to make the call. I watched over his shoulder.

Graciana was overjoyed to see Timothy, spat when Timothy told her his uncle Eddy had arranged his kidnapping, and eagerly agreed to contact Timothy's mother for him.

We all sighed in relief, but less than a minute later, Graciana called back, forehead creased with worry. "Anaximander will not put me through to Madam. He says she is unavailable; she has gone to the Spacer ship to negotiate your ransom."

"But I'm not on the Spacer ship! I'm free." Timothy looked horror-stricken. "It doesn't make any sense," he said after he'd disconnected. "The Spacers must be bluffing, pretending they have me when they don't."

It made sense to me. "Rianne, you have to contact your people. Tell them it's a trap. As soon as President Castellan boards their ship, Eddy will claim that they've killed her and attack the Spacers."

"But why?" Timothy asked.

Mike had figured it out. "Eddy wants the presidency."

Rianne didn't listen to any more. "I have to call my ship and warn them. You guys leave the room. I'm going to have a hard enough time convincing them as it is."

We left.

Five minutes later when Rianne wheeled herself out of the conference room, anxiety had tightened her skin. "They think I've been coerced. President Castellan is almost there. They won't listen to me. Unless . . ." Miserably, she looked at Timothy. "Unless they have some insurance."

Timothy took an involuntary step back. "No."

Rianne turned to Mike and me. "You have to help me. If I don't deliver Timothy to them, they'll fall into Eddy's trap."

Mike held up his hands. "Don't look at us. It has to be Timothy's decision."

"He won't do it." Guiltily, Rianne avoided looking at Timothy. "We'll have to take him captive. Give me the gun."

"How do you know he won't do it?" I asked. "You haven't asked him."

"Of course he won't do it," Rianne snapped.

"Ask him."

A long, painful moment passed. Rianne finally looked at Timothy. I was afraid she would ask him the wrong way, sarcastically, but she surprised me. "Please, Timothy. I know it's a lot to ask—"

It was more than a lot. Considering Timothy's past experience at the hands of Spacers, it was asking for the moon.

Timothy cut her off before she could beg. "I'll do it. On one condition."

"*Anything.*" Rianne's voice was intense.

"That as soon as you've delivered me, your part in this is over. You go to the beanstalk hospital on a stretcher and you do whatever the doctor tells you to do."

"The doctor's not going to be able to do anything more than the medication I already took, but
okay, I promise."

"I wasn't finished," Timothy said. "You also
have to let me pay for your treatment."

"That's two conditions," Rianne said.

Timothy folded his arms, looking stern.

"All right, you win. It's a deal." She struggled
with herself for a moment, then managed to grind
out, "Thank you."

We were too late.

We'd set the elevator to maximum speed, but it
had still taken another eight minutes to reach the
space station at the top of the beanstalk. Another
five minutes were spent discovering where the
Spacer ship was docked. We lost another minute
to an argument between Timothy and Rianne.
Timothy had refused to let her exert herself even
the tiny amount required to glide through zero-G
and insisted that she ride piggyback.

Altogether, eighteen minutes had passed by the
time we swung off the zero-G version of a motorized walkway—a lot of leather straps attached to a
moving track in the "ceiling"— and reached the
small, run-down spaceship that Rianne named as
our destination. Too late.

The Spacer man who opened the airlock said,
"Hurry up. President Castellan is demanding to
see her son. Jerome can't stall her much longer."

"I told him not to let her on board!" Rianne said
furiously from her position on Timothy's back.

The Spacer looked surprised. "Why would he do
that? A face-to-face meeting with SilverDollar's

president is what we've wanted all along. Someone with the authority to negotiate, not a flunky."

Eddy would have hated being called a flunky.

"Never mind, just hurry up and take us there," Rianne said.

Offended, the Spacer shoved off and glided inside the ship. He moved efficiently, guiding himself with the occasional touch.

The rest of us followed less gracefully as he took us down a curved corridor. At least I told myself it was a corridor. At odd moments my perspective would change, and I would feel as if we were falling down a well—albeit very slowly—or swimming up a tunnel. I preferred to think of it as a corridor.

Our guide turned left at the third intersection and opened the first hatch. He stayed outside while the four of us swam through. Rianne detached herself from Timothy's back. The people inside were oriented as if the hatchway was on the floor, not a wall, and my perspective shifted dizzyingly again.

"Timothy!" An avalanche of relief obliterated President Castellan's poker face. She let go of her handhold and launched herself at Timothy.

Her force sent them both bumping up against a wall, but she didn't seem to care, hugging him. "Are you all right?"

Timothy grabbed a handhold and steadied them both. "Yes, but—"

"He is fine, just as you were told," a smooth-voiced man, whom I took to be Jerome, interrupted. He had Asian features, but his skin was reddish, as if badly sunburned. Radiation? I wondered. One of his legs was hooked around the zero-G version of a chair, but the other leg ended at the knee.

"It is my wish that both of you will leave here in good health."

President Castellan's face hardened again at the blatant threat. "Yes, your good intentions are crystal clear to everyone," she said bitingly while clinging to the wall.

Jerome grew angry. "It's your company that's forced us to this."

"Mom." Timothy pulled at her arm. "We have to get out of here. Uncle Eddy's going to—"

President Castellan ignored her son, all her focus on annihilating the man who had stolen Timothy from her not once, but twice. "Nobody can force someone else to commit a criminal act. You're the one who abandoned morality—"

"Your hands are hardly lily-white. If the mines are closed down, my people will die."

"You exaggerate," President Castellan said coldly. "If such a decision were made, the Spacer population would be relocated to Earth free of charge."

Mike and I exchanged glances. This could go on for hours, and Eddy could strike at any moment.

"President Castellan," I said loudly, "look around you! Where are all the Spacers with silver eyes? Where are all the Augments SilverDollar paid for?"

Jerome looked impatient at the interruption, but President Castellan frowned. She looked around the room at Jerome and the four other Spacers hanging silently against the walls.

"Rianne, show her your heart."

Rianne scowled but obeyed, pulling down her neckline so that the trapdoor showed.

"Why weren't you given an Augmented heart?" President Castellan asked the very question that had been bothering me. I had a theory about the answer.

"Precisely my point," Jerome said. "Birth defects that are tolerable in zero-G will be crippling in Earth's gravity. I can move easily in space; on Earth I will be constrained to use canes and wheelchairs. Even if we wanted to, I and my people cannot return to Earth as easily as taking an elevator. Without Augments, Earth will kill us."

President Castellan's forehead wrinkled. "Yes, yes, I know. That's why I insisted on spending millions on Augments for Spacers even when the board of directors opposed me."

Jerome looked blank. The two of them were talking at cross-purposes. I intervened again.

"The Spacers never received the millions of dollars you budgeted for Augments for them." I spoke as if I knew it for a fact, not just a logical guess. "Eddy embezzled the money. And that's not all. Ask them how much ransom they received."

President Castellan's mouth fell open. "Is this true?" She turned to Jerome. "I paid two and a half million to get Timothy back."

Timothy stared at his mother in astonishment.

Jerome's eyes narrowed shrewdly. "We asked for one million. After months of negotiating, we settled for one hundred thousand dollars."

"He won't get away with it," President Castellan seethed. "I'll nail his carcass to the wall."

"But he *will* get away with it," Mike said.

"Unless we get out of here right now. In order to cover up his crime, Eddy needs all of us to die. He's going to attack and then tell the world it was a reprisal for the unprovoked killing of President Castellan and her son."

President Castellan turned to Jerome. "Release us, and as soon as I've cleaned house, we can talk about compensation. I'll forget about the kidnapping charges I should level against you."

It was a generous offer; I couldn't believe it when Jerome refused. "No. I have only your word Edward Castellan was responsible. SilverDollar has promised before and reneged. No one is released until you sign the Martian mines over to the Spacers." He indicated a paper held to a magnetic table.

"Like hell I will," President Castellan said.

CHAPTER

20

SHOUTS AND THE CRACK OF GUNFIRE from down the hall ended the argument. The attack had begun. Jerome and President Castellan were caught with their mouths open.

"Congratulations," Mike said angrily. "You just got yourselves killed."

"Eddy will have put Anaximander in charge of the strike force," I told Jerome. The irony would provide Eddy with more pulling-off-butterfly-wings fun. "Leave Anaximander to us." Anaximander wouldn't shoot Mike or me on sight. "Protect your hostages. I don't have time to convince you, but that is *not* a rescue mission out there."

"Think of it this way," Mike said. "You can't afford to be wrong. Rianne, hop on."

I pushed back into the corridor and began to pull myself hand over hand toward the sound of the battle.

"So what's our plan?" Rianne asked from Mike's back. "We ambush Anaximander?"

"No," Mike said. "We drown him."

We rounded a corner, and the gunshots got louder. As we stood there, two Spacers retreated past us, one bleeding bubbles of blood that floated away in zero-G.

"How many attackers?" I yelled as they went by.

"Six. Four robots and two men in armor." The injured Spacer and her companion had softguns but no body armor.

I waited for a break in the noise and then yelled: "Anaximander! Don't shoot. It's me, Angel." My voice echoed down the corridor, but Anaximander's Memory Recorder had a voice identification feature and the gunfire stopped.

"Angel? What are you doing here?"

"It's a long story—Mike's here, too. We're here to help you rescue Timothy and his mother."

Anaximander didn't confirm that he was there to rescue them. "Come out with your hands up, and we'll talk."

I went first, launching myself around the corner, both hands well away from my body. Mike followed with Rianne still on his back.

Anaximander didn't shoot. Neither did the two robots with him. Two, not four. The other armored man must have taken two robots and gone down a branching passageway. I could hear faint gunfire in the distance.

Both Anaximander and the robots were armed with blastguns. Blastguns used the same kind of bullets as softguns, but like machine guns, they were capable of firing many rounds per second. They weren't as safe; if fired point-blank at a wall, the wall would probably remain standing, but there would be holes in it.

From the quick look Mike shot me, I knew he'd noted the significance of the missing man and robots. We would have to act fast. There was a good chance that only Anaximander had been entrusted with the orders to kill President Castellan and Timothy, but Eddy might have other employees with Loyalty chips.

Anaximander flinched when he looked at Rianne—drowning, I hoped. The movement carried him back half a foot in zero-G. "Who's this?" he asked.

Rianne didn't take her eyes off Anaximander. I could sense her trying to find her father beneath the opaque silver gaze.

"An ally of ours, Rianne Pelletier," I said.

Another small stagger that zero-G exaggerated into a slow spin so that Anaximander had to grab a handhold to keep his blastgun pointed at us.

"She's a Spacer. Her father's name was Alexander," I said quickly, before Anaximander could speak.

This time there was no flinch; he didn't move at all, didn't blink, but his hand gripped the handhold fiercely.

He also didn't reprimand me for the irrelevant information I kept feeding him. I kept going, talking faster and faster: "Her father drowned in a bayou in Louisiana. He was one of the men who kidnapped Timothy the first time. His boat tipped, and he didn't know how to swim." And, finally, most devastatingly, "You're Rianne's father."

The last one did the trick. Anaximander curled up into a ball, hands coming up to cover his ears even though his helmet was in the way. His silver eyes were incapable of tears, but he threw back his head and keened in anguish. The sound sent a chill up my spine.

The robots watched impassively, frozen.

"Your wife's name was Francine. She loved you so much she engraved your name over her heart. Eddy made you watch your wife die." I sandbagged him with guilt.

"*Francine.*" Anaximander shuddered under another memory, another drowning. It was horrible to watch, like seeing a blind man walking through a minefield, setting off explosions with every misstep, but it was necessary.

When I had regained my memory, Mike had been there to hold and help me. With Anaximander, we couldn't take the chance of comfort. His Augments made him too lethal. We had to keep him drowning while we removed his chip.

When we unscrewed his helmet, his head came up, disoriented, but he sensed something was amiss. His hands combed the air in front of him, and he twisted away.

"Damn," Mike said, and sprang after him. I tried to hold Anaximander's head still, but he yanked my hands away, then pulled me back. His arm went around my neck in a headlock, choking me.

"Do you remember me?" Rianne floated in front of him. "I'm your daughter. The last time I saw you, I told you I hated you."

Anaximander's arms loosened and I pushed away, massaging my throat.

"I lied," Rianne continued. "I was mad at you because I knew you were going to risk your life for my sake and I was terrified you would die. Then, at the last minute, I yelled that I loved you, and you stopped to hug me. Do you remember?"

"Thatta girl," Mike said. "Almost there." His fingers sprang open the panel in Anaximander's skull that was used to access his Augments.

"When I was five, you had to miss my birthday party, but you recorded a birthday message for me. You sang me a little song, a stupid little song that you'd made up, which didn't even rhyme." She started to sing in a clear alto. " 'Happy birthday, Rianne/ I'm sorry I can't/ Be with you today/ I miss you every way.' " She called up memory after memory as we worked.

Unlike mine, Anaximander's Loyalty chip simply plugged into his other Augments. Instead of having to reset the chip's mode, all Mike had to do was locate it among the other Augments and pull the chip out. No surgery, no pain.

It was a small thing to have caused such harm. My first thought was to crush it, but Mike folded it up in tissue and pocketed it. "We need it for evidence."

I nodded and turned my attention to Anaximander—or rather Alexander—who was still curled into himself. I tried to pat his shoulder and ended up clutching his arm for balance. "It's not your fault. You aren't responsible for the actions the chip made you commit."

If he heard me, he gave no sign. It wasn't my

forgiveness that he needed. I signaled Rianne to come closer.

At first she didn't seem to know how to comfort him. She drifted just short of touching him, looking helpless. I was about to tell her to put her arms around him when her own reserve broke. "Daddy?"

His eyes opened. "Rianne. Baby." He pulled her to him in a close hug. Rianne clung just as tightly, and they spun slowly in place.

I had to look away. The moment felt too private.

I knew there would be problems and feelings for them to resolve later, but the first, biggest step had been taken.

Mike cleared his throat. "Sorry to interrupt, but Anaximander's partner might be closing in for the kill on Timothy and his mother right now."

Anaximander kept one arm around his daughter. "You know that? You know that this isn't a rescue mission?"

"We figured it out a little while ago," I said modestly. "Does your partner have a Loyalty chip, too?"

"No," Anaximander said, but I never got a chance to take my breath of relief. "The other man is Eddy. He said"—Anaximander's voice changed, became Eddy's voice, or rather a memory recording of Eddy's voice—" 'I'm tired of missing all the fun. I want to see my sister die. I want her to look into my eyes and know that I'm cleverer than she is.' " Anaximander's voice reverted to normal. "The fool."

Mike and I exchanged shark smiles over Eddy's unbelievable arrogance. "We'll catch him with his hands dirty," Mike said.

I got down to details. "How much firepower do

his robots have?" I asked Anaximander. "Should we take your robots with us? Will they obey you?"

"One of the robots is enough to kill everyone on the entire ship," Anaximander said grimly. He seemed steadier now that he had a task to do. "All of the robots will take orders from me, but Eddy's orders have priority. We'll need to take out their command nodes."

"And where are those?" I asked.

Anaximander demonstrated by putting a single bullet exactly between each of his robot's silver eyes. It was the closest I'd seen him come to bragging.

"Which way did Eddy go?" Rianne asked.

Anaximander pointed down a branching tunnel. As the four of us guided ourselves down it, the gunfire became heavier, a concussive throbbing that hurt my ears.

We stumbled over the remains of one of the robots. The Spacers had cut it in half. Its legs were still bouncing around aimlessly, while its torso clung to a handrail. Its blastgun was gone.

We saw more blood bubbles, but if any Spacers had been killed, their comrades had moved the bodies.

"Stay here while I go ahead alone," Anaximander said. "I have armor, and Eddy's expecting me."

I frowned. "Eddy has armor, too. What are you going to do when you find him? Tell me you're not going to confront him."

Anaximander said nothing, his silence an admission.

"You can't kill him," I said forcefully.

"Why not?" Rianne was totally on her father's side.

I scrambled to come up with a reason. "Because . . . he's the only one who knows where the stolen millions are. Without that money SilverDollar may be forced to shut down the Martian mines. All the Spacers will be out of work." Money usually left a trail, but my reasoning sounded good.

"Okay. I'll disarm him." Anaximander's voice was even, but something in his face made me uneasy, as if by "disarm" he meant "rip off Eddy's arm" rather than "take away Eddy's gun."

"I'll come with you," I announced. Before Mike and Rianne could protest being left behind, I handed Mike my gun. "You two set an ambush."

"Be careful," Mike said.

"I will."

Anaximander didn't wait a second longer. He raised his voice to a shout. "Sir, it's Anaximander." He pulled himself around the corner, leaving me to kick off after him and follow.

By the time I got there, Anaximander had already expertly shot the remaining robot. It tipped over backward and began a slow spin.

"What did you do that for?" Behind his transparent faceplate, Eddy looked put out.

"The Spacers have a device that disrupts their programming," Anaximander lied. His Augments gave him a definite advantage when it came to keeping a straight face. "My robots both malfunctioned and started firing wildly. They're now in the hands of the enemy. We need to abandon the mission."

"No. I'm too close." Eddy noticed me. "What's she doing here?"

"I tricked the terrorists into thinking I was one of them and talked them into sending me along with Timothy. He and President Castellan are being held back this way." I pointed.

"My, my, you have been busy." Eddy sounded paternally proud, as if I were a loyal dog who had performed some especially clever trick and now deserved a doggie biscuit.

"Come on," I said. "The Spacers might get nervous and kill the hostages."

Eddy hesitated, then smiled. "You first."

Was he suspicious? I couldn't tell.

My skin crawled at the thought of turning my back to him. Even though both Anaximander and I were free from the slavery of our chips, I was still afraid of Eddy. I told myself firmly that Eddy was no more dangerous than any other armed man— and probably a much poorer marksman—and started back around the corner to where Mike and Rianne waited in ambush.

At that point everything was still going well, but Eddy paused, one hand gripping a handhold, and looked at Anaximander, who had been staring at him expressionlessly. "Anaximander, I congratulate you on your training. It seems the student has surpassed the master." And he lifted his visor so he could pull the black butterfly token out from under his armor, taunting Anaximander, as it had always been safe for him to do in the past.

Anaximander snapped. He lunged forward, slamming Eddy into the tunnel wall. He ripped Eddy's gun away before Eddy could do more than blink. "You killed Francine!" He tore his wife's heart off Eddy's neck.

I threw myself onto Anaximander's back, but all I could do was float with him in zero-G. Anaximander ignored me and started pounding on Eddy, concentrating his blows on Eddy's unprotected face. "Help me!" I called to Mike.

"Do I have to?" Mike asked, but he braced his feet on the wall and pulled on Anaximander's waist while I pulled on Eddy. Even working together, the two of us couldn't budge them an inch. Anaximander's fists continued to fall, blackening one of Eddy's eyes and bloodying his nose. Eddy screamed and tried feebly to shield his face.

Anaximander bared his teeth in a primal smile, and behind him, Rianne echoed the expression. For the first time, I saw a father-daughter resemblance.

"You made me stand there and watch her die." Anaximander started to unscrew Eddy's helmet. "Now it's your turn to die."

"No. We need him to find the embezzled millions, remember? Francine would want the money to help the Spacers," I said.

My words penetrated. Breathing hard, Anaximander slowly released his victim. Eddy curled up in a ball. Anaximander loomed in front of him, menace exuding from every pore, Eddy's obscene necklace still clenched in his fist.

A glint of gold caught my eye, and I saw a broken necklace floating by one of the bulkheads. The more delicate gold chain must have been torn off Eddy's neck with the butterfly token.

On the chain floated a tiny golden angel.

Fear goose-stepped down my back. Eddy must

have taken the pendant the last time I'd seen him, when he'd asked if Timothy was violent.

Why couldn't I remember his taking it? Mike had restored the memories that had been blanked out by my Loyalty Induction. The pendant had disappeared afterward.

I realized then why I was so afraid of Eddy, and I started to move, but it was too late.

"Thanks for saving my life, Angel," Eddy croaked. *"Code fourteen."*

I went rigid.

The others didn't immediately understand what had happened.

"My Loyalty chip has been removed," Anaximander sneered. "The override code isn't going to help you now." He punched Eddy again.

But my chip hadn't been removed, only put in Passive mode. The override coded to Eddy's voice reactivated it. Helplessly, I froze in place, awaiting instructions.

"Kill them," Eddy gasped, clutching his nose. "Protect me."

CHAPTER

21

THE OVERRIDE WAS FIVE TIMES worse than the Loyalty chip's regular mode. It left my mind intact and aware but gave complete command of my body to Eddy.

If I'd had a gun, I would have shot them all—*bang, bang, bang.* Anaximander first, because he had threatened Eddy, then Mike, then Rianne.

Fortunately, Eddy's last command had been, "Protect me," so it took priority over "Kill them."

Eddy's blastgun was drifting up against a notch in the tunnel. I kicked up to the ceiling and had already snagged the gun by the time Mike figured out what was happening.

"She's under his control!" Mike yelled.

While I somersaulted back down in front of Eddy like a tigress defending its cubs, Anaximander pulled Rianne back around the corner.

Mike hesitated a moment longer. "Fight it, Angel!"

I fired off a burst, but my body was still moving from my earlier gymnastics and I missed by a foot.

Mike dove around the corner.

"What are you waiting for?" Eddy screamed, gesturing toward the tunnel.

My body started to move, but I stalled it by repeating his last command. Questions didn't count. "You told me to protect you. If I follow Mike, Anaximander might double back and kill you, moron."

Eddy puffed up with outrage. "What did you call me?"

"A moron." The override gave him command of my body, not my tongue. "You are a moron. And that wasn't your first mistake, either, you mental midget." The childish taunts felt incredibly good.

"Don't insult me again." A command. "I don't think I care for your attitude," Eddy said coldly. He pinched the bridge of his nose to stop the bleeding. "When this is over, I think I'll make some changes."

Ice filled my spinal column. In override mode, Eddy could play with me like a doll. If he told me to jump off a cliff, I would do it.

"I'm wearing body armor; I'm perfectly safe," Eddy said inaccurately; he wasn't safe as long as his visor was up. "Go after them now."

I obeyed, cursing inwardly, but a moment later he took the bait. "Wait! Tell me what mistake you think I made."

"Mistakes, plural. You haven't told me who is my primary target or what to do after I kill them."

"Anaximander's your primary target, Mike is secondary. Forget the girl. She wasn't armed, and she's crippled."

Which just went to prove how stupid he was.

Mike would smile at Eddy's funeral, and Anaximander might kill him in the heat of anger, but Rianne was the one capable of drilling a hole in his heart while he slept. I happily followed his command and blanked all thought of Rianne from my mind.

"After you kill them, come help me hunt down my sister and her brat. It's too bad I can't be in two places at once. I'd love to watch you blow away your boyfriend. Oh, yes, Michael Vallant used to be your boyfriend, didn't you know?" He was trying to hurt me by engaging my drowning reflex.

I left him puzzled by my lack of response.

Override mode made no allowance for caution. I pulled myself along the tunnel as fast as I could one-handed, finger on the trigger, alert, not knowing if I was the cat or the mouse.

While I trusted Mike to shoot to wound even with his own life in jeopardy, Anaximander was another matter entirely. He was a Spacer. The stakes were higher for him.

One of the hatches I passed wasn't completely closed. I saw Rianne hiding inside, then, as commanded, promptly forgot that I'd seen her and kept going.

Around the next corner, I saw something red ahead of me—Mike's shirt—and fired even as my eyes registered that it was just a piece of cloth.

The recoil threw me violently backward, and Rianne snatched the blastgun out of my hands. I immediately forgot her again as I thumped the back of my head and skinned one elbow on the wall before bouncing off again. Debris pelted by me.

Then Mike attacked from above, catching my wrists and holding them fast.

We banged around in the narrow tunnel. "Don't let go," I panted, even as the chip made me squirm like an eel.

"Never," Mike swore.

My feet touched a wall, and I kicked off with all my strength, smashing Mike against a protruding bulkhead. "No!" I cried out, anguished, as he let go of my wrists.

Then Anaximander grabbed me from behind and pinned my arms against my body. Mike uncurled from the wall and gamely tackled my legs, immobilizing them. I noticed that Mike's forehead was bleeding and knew that I had done that. Guilt choked me, even as I fought furiously.

Rianne said something and waved a blastgun in my direction, but I forgot about her and her threat as soon as I heard it and continued to thrash.

"Code one." Anaximander's lips moved, but it was Eddy's voice that I heard. "Code five."

Anaximander was apparently searching through his Memory Recorder's vast library of conversations with Eddy, scanning for numbers, because he called out numbers in random order, "Code seventeen, code seven, code thirty," instead of a one, two, three progression.

"Code fourteen."

I stopped fighting and went limp. "That did it. Thanks, you guys."

Mike grinned, cute even while bleeding, and released his hold on my legs.

My foot lashed out, aiming for Mike's vulnerable throat, but Anaximander jerked me backward, preventing the blow from connecting.

Mike's face whitened, but he soon had me pinned again.

"Code fifty," Anaximander droned. "Code fifty-one, code fifty-two . . ."

Despair clenched my heart. There were too many numbers still to go through. Eddy might find Timothy by the time I was released.

"Code thirty-two."

I relaxed. "That one did it, guys. For real this time." I smiled, but Mike and Anaximander didn't believe me.

And they were right not to. We had to go through the whole depressing process four more times before hitting it right with code twenty-four.

I knew immediately because I stopped forgetting Rianne. She had a foot hooked through one of the wall handholds and was holding both blast-guns. Her heart seemed to be holding up so far.

"Okay, I'm free, and I can prove it. Anaximander, command me to do something in Eddy's voice."

"Don't kill us," Anaximander said instantly.

Mike swore in disgust. "You couldn't have thought of that a bit earlier?"

Anaximander refrained from pointing out that Mike hadn't thought of it either. "Don't open your mouth." The words came out jerkily, four words from different sentences replayed separately.

I opened my mouth wide.

"Good enough for me," Mike said. He released my legs, and Anaximander let go of my arms.

Rianne wasn't quite so trusting; one blastgun remained leveled at my gut.

I ignored her, focusing on Mike. I'd almost killed him. I held his hand. Squeezed it. "Thank you. Again."

"It's not your fault," Mike said, reading my mind.

"I know." But it felt like my fault. Eddy had installed Loyalty chips in all three of us, but I'd been the only one affected by the override. I felt as though I should have been able to resist, too—however stupid that was.

"I should have taken you to a surgeon." Mike's grim face made me realize I wasn't the only one who felt guilty. "Made the UN pay up like what's-his-face promised you."

"You can assign blame later," Anaximander said. "We have to capture Eddy." He retrieved both blastguns from Rianne. "You stay here and tell Jerome what's happening. Mike, Angel, let's go."

Rianne didn't look happy, muttering, "Yes, Dad," but she stayed behind.

"What's our plan? Eddy's armor will protect him from our blastguns," I said as we backtracked down the corridor.

Anaximander hesitated. "A hail of bullets won't kill him, but it might smash him against a wall hard enough to knock him out. It's our best chance."

My blood chilled, but I made myself speak. "No, it's not. Innocent people could get killed if the two of you start blasting away at each other in your armor. Plus, you might rupture the hull. Our best plan is to send me in alone. I'll tell Eddy I killed you both, then take him by surprise and disarm him."

Mike nodded reluctantly. "You're right. You're the only one he won't shoot on sight. But you'll have to be careful. As soon as Eddy realizes you're free, he'll activate the override again."

"I can fix that," Anaximander said. "Code fourteen. Don't. Obey. My." A pause while he searched for the right word. "Commands. Code twenty-four."

"Great." I smiled in relief. "I hate—"

"Code fourteen," Anaximander said, double-checking, and I stopped smiling because the override command overrode the previous command not to obey Eddy.

Mike read that truth on my face. "Hell."

"Code twenty-four," Anaximander said, and I was free again.

All of us were unhappy, but our options were severely limited. The plan had to stand as it was.

Anaximander contacted Rianne on his palmtop. "Where's Eddy?"

Rianne came through. "According to the latest reports, he's in the cargo bay. He's getting close to finding Timothy and his mother. They're hiding in some containers."

It took five long minutes to reach the entrance to the cargo bay, but Eddy was still busy blasting containers when we peeked through the door. He must not have found Timothy and President Castellan yet. From the looks of the exploded water containers, he was getting frustrated.

Mike stopped me before I could expose myself by going through the door. He kissed me twice, one fierce and one sweet. "You can beat him."

I hung onto his neck a moment longer than was necessary. I was afraid that the next time I saw him, I might have to shoot him.

I called up the memory of how I'd felt when the chip had made me shoot Mike, set my face into lines of sorrow and murderous hate, then pulled myself through the doorway into the cargo bay.

Eddy was only ten feet away, and he saw me immediately. His avid gaze drank in my pain like a parasite latching on to flesh. "Did you kill them for me, my angel? Did you kill your teacher and your boyfriend?"

"Yes," I gritted out. "Someday— Someday." The words were a promise that made Eddy smile. He didn't know someday was today. I dodged water bubbles and floating debris, moving closer to Eddy.

"Once this is over I'll have to get you to tell me all the little details. It's a shame about Anaximander," Eddy said carelessly. "He was useful to have around. But I suppose I have you now."

He smiled. The sight made me shudder. "I hate you." I glared. Eddy would expect such clichés.

"Poor Angel." Eddy was almost purring. "You'd kill me if you could, wouldn't you?"

"Yes." Well, disarm him anyhow. I calculated the meter and a half of distance between us. If I pushed off hard from the floor, I should have enough speed to rip the blastgun from Eddy as I went by, but then what? There was no way to dispose of the weapon before Eddy called out my override code.

"Opening each crate is taking too long." Eddy

frowned, then raised his voice. "This is your five-second warning. Come out now, or I'll blow you to smithereens. One. Two."

Don't fall for it, I thought. *He's bluffing. He wants to see your faces.*

"Three. Four. Five."

Eddy aimed at one of the crates. I was about to make a try for his gun, when President Castellan's nerve broke. "Stop! I'm in here." Her voice came from a crate two over from the one Eddy had targeted.

"Open the crate," Eddy said to me.

I thumbed open the latches and raised the lid, gambling that Eddy would want to gloat a little, not just kill his sister on the spot.

President Castellan emerged. Her hair was in disarray, but she showed no fear. "Hello, Edward."

His triumph instantly turned to rage. "Don't call me that!"

She shrugged. "As you prefer. I've always thought Eddy was a little boy's name, not a man's. But then you never grew up, did you, Eddy? You see something you want and you grab it, without thinking about the consequences. You embezzled the money earmarked for Spacer Augments and squandered it on toys. You might have gotten away with it once, but you got greedy. You stole all the money, and the Spacers began to complain. You created a mess, and ever since you've been scrambling frantically to clean it up. Now you're going to kill me. But killing me will just make a bigger mess. A murder investigation this time. The UN will be all over you like a rash. You'll never be president of anything larger than a jail cell."

"Shut up." Face full of rage, Eddy jabbed the blastgun in her direction.

I watched his trigger finger anxiously. If I sprang at him now, the gun might go off.

"And if I don't shut up? What will you do? Kill me? Some threat. You're already going to do that." President Castellan looked scornful.

Eddy bared his teeth. "Yes, I am. But first I'm going to make you watch while I kill your precious legacy, your son. Angel, cuff her to a crate, then start opening the rest. When you find Timothy, bring him to me."

President Castellan tried to resist, but I was stronger and quicker. She was cuffed to the handle of a crate within a matter of seconds. "Sorry," I told her. "I don't want to do this. He's controlling me with a Loyalty chip."

"Stop chatting, and hurry up!"

I moved to the closest crate and flipped up the lid. Timothy stared up at me with terror-wide eyes. "This one's empty." I shut the lid before he started to float out.

President Castellan didn't overtly react, but from the new tension in her body I knew that she knew I was lying. "Beanstalk security will have called the UN by now. If you surrender now, you might go to jail for only a few years instead of the rest of your life." She moved slightly, pulling Eddy's attention to her to give me a chance.

"How stupid do you think I am? I won't go to jail, if all the witnesses are dead and can't be questioned under TrueFalse," Eddy said.

"It's not that you're stupid," President Castellan said dispassionately as I maneuvered myself to the side and behind Eddy with a series of small pushes. I flipped up more lids. "It's that you're lazy."

I launched myself at Eddy. My feet hit him in the middle of his back, knocking him into a spin. Before he could react, I tore the gun from his grasp and bounded up off the floor. But the exit was too far away, and I knew it.

Where the hell were Mike and Anaximander? I'd done my job. I'd disarmed Eddy.

Any moment now Eddy was going to call out my override code and command me to stop. I tried to distract him by aiming the blastgun at the breastplate of his golden armor—

And my finger stuck in the trigger.

I couldn't pull the trigger. No matter how I struggled, my finger wouldn't move that last quarter inch.

Eddy began to laugh. He laughed and laughed, giggling helplessly, while I watched in dawning horror. "Poor Angel," he gasped at last. "You weren't expecting that, were you? I've been playing a trick on you."

I remembered the way I'd been unable to perceive Rianne after Eddy commanded me to "forget" her. "What did you do to me?" I demanded, but I knew. Sometime since I'd entered the cargo bay, Eddy had invoked my override command. Then later he'd commanded me to forget that he'd done so, setting up his "joke."

"I said, 'code fourteen,' as soon as you entered the cargo bay," Eddy said. He was all but dancing, he was so pleased with himself. "This whole time you thought you were acting only on your own initiative. Who's the moron now, huh?"

I swallowed. "What did you do to me?"

"Which time?" Eddy grinned nastily. "The first time I used your override was back at the Operations facility."

The time Anaximander had tried to prevent Eddy from talking to me alone and had walked into a wall.

"I commanded you to act like a chicken. You flapped your wings and cock-a-doodle-dooed and tried to lay an egg."

I flushed with humiliation and dread. I couldn't remember acting like a chicken—Eddy had obviously used the override to wipe out my memory of the episode—but it was after that that Shadow Angel had started to fear him.

"The second time was at Timothy's convention when I talked to you alone upstairs. You told me all about your plans to give Timothy some fun by taking him to the planetarium, and then—" Eddy stopped maliciously, letting my mind imagine all sorts of horrible things. Had he made me beg? Crawl? Kiss him?

I rose to the bait. "What did you make me do?"

"I'll give you a hint," Eddy said. "Did you have a stomachache afterward?"

I frowned, couldn't remember.

"You ate a paper plate," Eddy said. "I told you to think it was a cupcake and eat it. Then for dessert you ate some of my pocket lint."

"And this time?" I asked.

Another snake-slither grin. "Well, I was a little upset with you for not doing as you were told and killing Anaximander and your boyfriend. So I made you break your finger."

I looked down at my hands and saw immediately that my left little finger was red and swollen, but I couldn't feel any pain. It wasn't even numb; it felt perfectly normal.

"I commanded you not to feel the pain," Eddy said. "It would have spoiled the joke. But the joke's over now. Feel again."

I gasped in agony, tears springing into my eyes, as my broken finger screamed back to life.

"Leave her alone, you sadistic creep," President Castellan said, outraged on my behalf.

Eddy smiled as he turned his attention back to her. "Did you think you were going to be rescued? Sorry. Now then, I commanded Angel not to attack me until after she'd found Timothy so he must be in one of those three crates there." He pointed, then turned to me. "Angel, shoot—"

I fired the blastgun before Eddy could command me to shoot Timothy. I fired into the air with the muzzle right next to my ear and the shot temporarily deafened me. The recoil propelled me backward and sent jagged pain streaking up my finger. I screamed and deliberately kept on screaming.

Eddy's mouth opened. He shouted. But I didn't hear him and therefore didn't have to obey.

I threw the blastgun away, buying time. Eddy lunged toward me, and I flung myself sideways out of reach, yelling with all my might, fingers in my ears.

Two, three, four bodies dived past me. Mike and Anaximander and several Spacers tackled Eddy, immobilizing him and unscrewing his helmet. Without his armor and his invulnerability, Eddy lost interest in fighting. He surrendered.

He looked around for me, but Mike slapped a sticky-gag over his mouth before he could yell any more commands.

Just to be on the safe side, I stayed where I was until they took him away.

Four minutes later Anaximander freed me. "Code twenty-four."

"Thanks." I could have asked him to put me back under override command again and tell me to stop feeling my finger, but I decided that I preferred the pain.

CHAPTER

22

THE NEXT FEW HOURS were total chaos.

Mike stayed with me while I got my finger splinted and numbed, and then we rejoined the main group. We got there just in time to see five UN police officers arrest Eddy.

They removed his sticky-gag. Anaximander and Mike floated on either side of me, ready to act if Eddy invoked the override, but he wasn't quite stupid enough to incriminate himself in front of UN police.

"It's about time you got here," Eddy complained. "Those people kidnapped my nephew, Timothy Castellan. I came here to rescue him."

"No, you didn't!" Timothy shrilled. "You tried to kill Mom and me!"

I happened to glance at President Castellan at that moment and saw the tearful joy on her face. I wondered how long it had been since Timothy called her "Mom."

Eddy looked at Timothy with pity. "Is that what

your kidnappers told you? It's a lie. How could you even think that about me? After all the baseball games I've taken you to?"

President Castellan put her hand on Timothy's shoulder and pulled him away. "Don't waste your breath on him. We're telling the truth, and TrueFalse will bear us out."

Eddy's smooth expression curdled. "Your persecution of me is going to hurt you at the next board meeting," he shouted after her. "Don't think I won't be there. My lawyer will get me out of these in two shakes." He held up his handcuffs.

President Castellan kept her back to him.

I shook my head. Eddy actually seemed to believe that he still had a place at SilverDollar, that his lawyer could somehow make the money he'd embezzled and the Loyalty chips he'd installed disappear. He'd probably never been in trouble before that he couldn't bribe his way out of. President Castellan was right; he'd never grown up.

Eddy must have continued spewing accusations, because police officers soon arrested Jerome.

I knew other arrests would follow, everything coming out under TrueFalse. Both Anaximander and Rianne had committed a crime and might go to jail. With luck, a jury would rule that they had already been punished enough, but I thought that neither Anaximander nor Rianne would mind paying the price of a few years in prison since Timothy's kidnappings had ultimately resulted in Augments for their people.

At President Castellan's request, the police officer left off Jerome's handcuffs and merely guarded the hatchways while she and Jerome got down to some serious business.

"The Augments are our first priority," President Castellan said. "I'll need data on who needs what and which cases are the most serious. Edward was in charge of the entire Martian mining operation so all the information I have on file is suspect. He may have inflated claims in order to embezzle more money."

"We have our own records; I can get you that information."

"Excellent," President Castellan said briskly. "Now, on to finances. Edward's accounts will be frozen until after his trial; it may be a year or two before SilverDollar regains whatever remains of the funds he embezzled."

Jerome started to draw himself up, to protest.

President Castellan held up a hand. "I can promise you five million immediately for the worst cases. I can get that out of emergency funds; the rest I'll have to argue out of the board of directors."

I tuned out as the conversation turned to more boring budget details.

Rianne brought Mike, Timothy, and me sandwiches, then hung around the edges of the meeting. "What's happening?" she whispered as we all chowed down.

Instead of answering her, Timothy looked at her reproachfully. "What are you doing here? You promised me you'd go to the hospital."

"There was a line," Rianne said defensively. "Eddy injured a few people, you know."

"They should have received treatment by now,"

Timothy said. "Come with me. You're going to the doctor right now." He left his sandwich floating in midair, took her arm in a firm grip, and started towing her to the door.

"But I want to find out what happens!" Rianne complained.

"Mike and Angel will give you a full report," Timothy promised, undeterred.

My lips twitched, but I didn't go to Rianne's rescue. I suspected she enjoyed Timothy's concern.

The discussion between President Castellan and Jerome had heated up. Now they were discussing the fate of the Martian mines. Jerome was pushing for a promise, and President Castellan wasn't giving it.

"Once your people receive the Augments they need, they're no longer trapped in space. They can live on Earth if they'd like."

"But we don't like." Jerome chopped his hands through the air. "We want to stay in space."

"No decision has been made to close the mines," President Castellan said. "But the economic climate is changing. If SilverDollar doesn't change with it, we'll go bankrupt and the mines will shut down anyhow. Then where will you be?"

"Then sign the mines over to us," Jerome said stubbornly. "We'll keep them going."

"Now, that truly isn't possible," President Castellan said. "You're forgetting that SilverDollar doesn't own the mines. We just have a lease. You need to talk to the UN about negotiating your own lease."

Jerome's jaw dropped.

I couldn't resist. "Or you might want to talk to

the UN about taking out a loan and terraforming Mars."

Jerome blinked. That seemed to be a new idea, too.

President Castellan shook his hand, an awkward push-me pull-me motion in zero-G. "I need to go now and start setting in motion some of the things we discussed. I'm sure we'll talk again soon."

The police took Jerome away. Mike and I started to push off, but President Castellan stopped us. "Angel, Mike, you're next on my list."

"For what?" I asked warily.

"SilverDollar takes no responsibility for the Loyalty chips Edward inflicted on both of you against your will, *but*," President Castellan emphasized, "we would like to repair some of the damage he caused. We will pay for the surgery to remove both your chips as well as psychological counseling, should you need it. Loyalty chips are ugly, ugly things. Edward used you in the worst possible way."

I shrugged. It hadn't been pleasant, but Shadow Angel had helped me keep some self-respect. I would recover.

President Castellan went on. "We'll also sponsor a year of college education for both of you. In return, you'll sign an agreement, promising not to sue us."

"Well," Mike said smiling, "let's talk about that, shall we?"

I left them to it, retreating to a corner and turning on my palmtop. I wanted to know if Mike and I had been mentioned on the news or, even worse, identified as Renaissance children. To my relief, so far the whole thing was being reported only as "unexplained gunfire on the space station."

While searching through news channels, I saw a clip of Zinnia and Dahlia. Both of them were crying their eyes out and hugging. The reporter announced that the Cartwright clones had been reunited after the Sons and Daughters of the Stars terrorist group had kidnapped one of them.

Zinnia refused to comment on her "harrowing experience," but when they asked Dahlia about the size of the ransom she had paid to get her fellow clone back, she said, "I'd have to be an idiot to tell you that, but I will say this: if anyone touches my sister again they'll have me to deal with."

My palmtop chirped, announcing that I had an incoming message. I pressed Accept, and a recording of my parents appeared on the screen.

My mother had obviously been crying recently, and my own eyes pricked in response. "Angel," Mom said, and stopped, one hand held out in entreaty.

Dad took over. "Thank you for your message. We understand why you hadn't called before, but we've been worried about you. You can reach us at the following places." He gave me their address and vidphone number. "When the publicity dies down, we hope that you'll come back to us, but Dr. Hatcher says he'll relay messages if that's safer for you. We love you very much." Dad started to look a bit teary-eyed, too. "Take care. You'll always have a home with us."

I bit my bottom lip and immediately replayed the recording. Except for the emotional strain, both my mom and dad looked well. I wondered if they'd received their family license, if they'd landed acting roles as they'd dreamed.

I wanted quite badly to call them, but right now was the wrong time.

If Mike and I continued to live on the run from those who wanted to exploit or kill the violet-eyed, I wasn't sure if there would ever be a right time. I thought long and hard about that as I waited for Mike to finish negotiating with President Castellan.

Mike was smiling when he and President Castellan emerged from their corner. He shook hands with her, then drifted over to me. "I got it," he said, flashing me a plastic card. "A lump sum of cash, instead of sponsoring our education. We've got what we came for, money and identicards. I say we split before the cops get around to asking us questions."

He looked restless, and I remembered his fear that the UN would try to "put a leash on us."

I thought about splitting, then shook my head. I was starting to think we had done the wrong thing in not sticking around after Dr. Frankenstein's death. "Let's stay."

"What?" Mike looked astonished.

I turned all my persuasion on Mike. "If you want to run again, I'll go with you. That's not an issue. But I want to accept Dr. Hatcher's offer to go into a protection program for Renaissance children." I took a deep breath. "I want more than just identicards and money. I want the chip out of my head for good. It's true that we could buy new identities with the money President Castellan is going to give us—finish high school, go to college, have careers—but we'd always be looking over our shoulders, afraid of being recognized, afraid to make friends. I want to stay friends with Timothy and Rianne. I miss Wendy—she was my best friend back in Chinchaga. I want to find out if she's forgiven her father and if she's still dating Carl. I want to see my parents again."

Beside me Mike tensed, a silent protest, and I held his hand. "Will you at least talk to Dr. Hatcher?"

"Yes, but it won't change anything," Mike said. "Dr. Hatcher may be the great guy you think he is, but what if he isn't? What if he's setting another trap, or the UN wants us to spy for them?"

"Then we escape again. It's not like we haven't done it before," I said wryly. "We'll survive."

Mike laughed, relaxing. "That's true. Okay, Angel, go ahead and call your Dr. Hatcher. We'll give him the benefit of the doubt."

I kissed him in thanks and then began to dial. More than anything, I wanted to learn to trust again.

About the Author

Nicole Luiken was born May 25, 1971. She grew up on a farm in northern Alberta (latitude 57° N). She wrote her first novel at age thirteen (it was summer holidays and there was nothing else to do). She is the author of *Violet Eyes*, which begins the story of Angel and Michael, as well as three other young adult novels (*Unlocking the Doors, The Catalyst,* and *Escape to Overworld*) and one adult thriller (*Running on Instinct*). She lives in Edmonton, Alberta, with her husband, Aaron Humphrey, and young son, Simon. It is physically impossible for her to go without writing for more than three days in a row. Nicole's Web site is www.geocities.com/nmluiken.

FAT BOY SAVES WORLD

A wonderfully weird novel by **Ian Bone**

Susan Bennett, sixteen-year-old boarding school
reject, shaves her head and returns home to her
parents' mansion. It's the scene of many battles,
watched over by her bloated older brother. His
name is Neat, and he hasn't uttered a word for
eight years. But Susan's parents are away, and
Neat has a little surprise: he speaks and says, "I
want to save the world."

With the help of Todd, a young street actor who
believes in people and possibilities, Neat goes
on local cable TV and dispenses advice. Then,
when Susan's parents return home, she decides
the time has come to face up to them—and her
life. What does she really want? And how can
she connect with Todd, whose kindness and
affection she really craves?

Available from Pocket Pulse
Published by Pocket Books

#3121

BASED ON THE HIT TV SERIES

Prue, Piper, and Phoebe Halliwell
didn't think the magical incantation
would really work. But it did.
Now Prue can move things with her
mind, Piper can freeze time, and
Phoebe can see the future. They are
the most powerful of witches—
the Charmed Ones.

**Available from Pocket Pulse
Published by Pocket Books**

. . . A GIRL BORN
WITHOUT THE FEAR GENE

FEARLESS™

A SERIES BY
FRANCINE PASCAL

FROM POCKET PULSE
PUBLISHED BY POCKET BOOKS

3029

In 1897 the renowned polar explorer Robert Peary sailed into New York harbor with six Eskimos as his "cargo." He deposited them at the American Museum of Natural History as "living specimens" and then abandoned them. Four Eskimos died within a year. One returned to Greenland. Only Minik, a boy of six or seven, remained.

During his twelve years in New York, Minik learned English, played sports, and acquired a taste for big-city life. But all that ended when he found his father's skeleton on display at the museum. Disillusioned and desperate to return to his people, Minik finally sailed for Greenland in 1909. He relearned his native language and hunting skills, and even assisted a new generation of polar explorers, yet the rest of his life became a search to find a place where he truly belonged.

**AVAILABLE FROM ARCHWAY PAPERBACKS
PUBLISHED BY POCKET BOOKS**

3088